Kyle had no words to express his love

Instead he opted for a kiss. Gentle, poignant, the kiss set the tone for their lovemaking. Without ending it, he guided Meredith to the bed. Still kissing her, he slid his hands under her T-shirt and pushed it up, caressing her flesh as he bared it.

He longed for the right words to express his feelings, but words of love did not come easily to him. He was better with snaps and zippers than with words, and slowly undressed her.

Kyle watched Meredith's face as their bodies joined. They kissed deeply while their entwined bodies searched frenetically for the complementary rhythms that would release them from the delicious torment of desire driving them....

Afterward, he held her in his arms. He wanted to tell her how much being with her meant to him. He wanted to tell her about the different ways he needed her in his life, but words of endearment, so long out of use, stuck in his throat.

He fell asleep with love and hope strong in his heart. But when he awoke, Meredith was gone....

Glenda Sanders loves to pack her stories with emotion. That is certainly the case in *A Human Touch*, which tackles the issue of homelessness. When you look at the homeless as individuals, Glenda declares, you are forced to see that many of them are victims of circumstances far beyond their control. Glenda movingly illustrates that point in the love story of Kyle and Meredith. The contrast between her own life and that of her heroine made Glenda very aware of how blessed she has been.

Books by Glenda Sanders

HARLEQUIN TEMPTATION

A Human Touch
GLENDA SANDERS

Harlequin Books

TORONTO • NEW YORK • LONDON
AMSTERDAM • PARIS • SYDNEY • HAMBURG
STOCKHOLM • ATHENS • TOKYO • MILAN

'Tis the human touch in this world that counts,
    The touch of your hand and mine,
Which means far more to the fainting heart
    Than shelter and bread and wine;
For shelter is gone when the night is o'er,
    And bread lasts only a day,
But the touch of the hand and the sound of the voice
    Sing on in the soul alway.

Spencer Michael Free
The Human Touch and Other Poems

Published July 1991

ISBN 0-373-25456-3

A HUMAN TOUCH

1

LIZARDS SCURRIED OUT of Kyle Sawyer Brooks's path as he followed the fieldstone sidewalk to the rectory door. A push of the doorbell button set off a flurry of chimes inside the house. Kyle stood in the crystalline air so characteristic of Orlando winters, pondering Mark's urgent summons while he waited.

What had prompted Mark to call? And why had he been so evasive on the phone? Though he and Mark had once been as close as brothers, in recent years theirs had not been a relationship in which either of them would pick up the phone and suggest an impromptu get-together.

Mark himself opened the door. "Thanks for coming so quickly."

Brushing past him, Kyle asked, "What'd you expect me to do after that phone call?" Mark's conversation had been peppered with *i* words: *imperative . . . immediately . . . important.*

Kyle waited for an explanation. Since Mark appeared disinclined to offer one, Kyle demanded bluntly, "What the hell's going on, Mark? And don't raise that censuring eyebrow at me, *Father*— I knew you when you could outswear me, remember?"

Kyle and Mark had shared a childhood filled with Little League baseball and outdoor basketball, and had wiled away hot Florida summers playing in the Darbys' backyard swimming pool. As teenagers, they had learned to drive in the same class, drunk their first beers together and double-dated to the homecoming and prom dances. In undergraduate school, they'd been roommates in their first apartment.

Even after graduation, when Mark shocked Kyle by entering the seminary and Kyle enrolled in law school, they'd remained close—until Shannon died.

Mark laughed away Kyle's ill humor. "I should invite you over more often, Kyle. You could help keep me humble."

Kyle ran his fingers through his hair. "Don't start in with the religious jargon, Mark. We go too far back for that. Just tell me what's so important that I had to drop everything and come running over here."

His lips compressed in irritation, Mark hesitated a second before replying, "It's not so much what, as who." His tone was oppressively serious. "I have a case for you, Kyle. One that's right up your alley."

"*Pro bono publico*, no doubt," Kyle said, and Mark's sheepish expression confirmed the hunch. Frowning, Kyle asked, "Since when does a priest call in a divorce attorney?"

"It's not a divorce case," Mark told him. "You've handled some—what do they call it?—*palimony* cases, haven't you?"

"Weirder and weirder," Kyle responded drolly.

"And paternity and child support cases?"

"Yes," Kyle acknowledged. "I've handled cases like that."

Then Mark continued solemnly, "If ever I've seen a case demanding justice, it's the one I called you about."

Kyle was just about to start firing questions at Mark, when Mark raised his hand to stop him. "Later. First, let's get something to drink."

Kyle followed Mark down a hallway, past a formal dining room and bookcase-lined study into an old-fashioned country kitchen. A young woman was seated in the dinette, with a steaming bowl of soup and a plate of cheese and crackers on the table in front of her. She glanced up, then quickly lowered her eyes to her soup.

The woman wasn't dirty, but she was unkempt. Her hair hung in shapeless, uncombed straggles. Even makeup, had she been wearing any, could not have disguised the pallor or gauntness of her face. Her whole attitude was one of resignation, of having given up. It showed in the droop of her shoulders and in the way she'd averted her gaze, not wanting to look directly at the two men.

Numerous expressions came to Kyle's mind, all of them implying defeat: *hangdog, down-and-out, rode hard and put away wet*. Obviously, she was one of Mark's "causes."

Kyle sucked in a breath and hoped that she wasn't the cause Mark was going to try to saddle *him* with. His practice kept him up to his armpits in desperate, embittered women, but they plopped down hefty retainers before he started listening to their sad stories and handing them tissues.

"Hello, Meredith," Mark greeted in an even voice.

"Father," the woman murmured into her soup.

"This is a friend of mine," Mark continued. "Kyle Brooks. Kyle, this is Meredith."

"Hello," Kyle said.

The woman looked up briefly, more in Kyle's direction than at Kyle directly. Her gray eyes, red-rimmed, had a haunted, pained quality. Again, she quickly diverted her gaze. "Hello."

Mark opened the refrigerator door and turned to Kyle. "How about a beer?"

"Oh?" Kyle replied distractedly. "Sure. Whatever you've got."

Mark tossed him a can in a gesture that took both of them back to their college years, when they had shared a modest apartment and many a beer and pizza. They'd still been best friends then, not yet anticipating becoming brothers-in-law; innocent of how cruelly fate could twist lives.

"Would you like a beer, Meredith?" Mark asked.

"No, thank you," she answered softly. "I'm nursing. Alcohol's not good for the baby."

As if on cue, a soft snuffling sound rose from a chair next to Meredith's. Kyle tracked the sound to an infant carrier, where a baby gasped in its sleep. Meredith leaned over to touch the baby's cheek with her fingertip and made a soothing sound. The baby made a little suckling gesture, then settled back into peaceful slumber.

"We'll be in my study if you need us," Mark told her, gesturing to Kyle that he should follow him.

Kyle sat down in the chair facing Mark's desk. Mark dropped into his own chair and popped the top of his beer, ignoring the scowl on Kyle's face.

"What the hell are you trying to sucker me into?" Kyle challenged.

Mark responded with infuriating calm. "That's the second time you've alluded to hell."

"Cut the sanctimonious crap. You called me over here as though it were a matter of life and death, then stroll me into the kitchen and toss a beer at me as if you'd asked me to come over and watch a game on TV. What gives?"

"Hell is an interesting concept," Mark said. "Some people think of it very literally—a place of eternal punishment. Others use the word to mean any unpleasant place or state. Hell on earth, so to speak."

Kyle grimaced, growing more and more irritated with Mark's deliberate obtuseness.

"If you're referring to the latter concept," Mark continued, "that of hell created by man, then I'd say the woman you just met has been about as close to hell as you can get on this earth."

"If you're trying to impress me, don't," Kyle retorted. "You're not going to tell me anything I probably haven't heard before. Especially if there's a man at the root of her problems."

Mark smiled enigmatically and stared at Kyle in a way that made him uneasy. "I don't believe you're as calloused as you'd like me to believe you are."

It seemed to Kyle that Mark was peering straight inside him, seeing all his foibles and the guilt that sometimes threatened to consume him. "You're a priest," he told Mark. "It's your obligation to search for the good in people."

"You're disillusioned, Kyle, but no matter how much you've changed, you're not cruel. You'll never convince me you can be deliberately cruel."

"Life is cruel," Kyle said. "I manage to survive."

Mark let the comment pass without reply and took a long draft of beer. "The woman you just met came into the church this afternoon looking for help. She's been living in her car, eating peanut butter to keep up her strength. Yesterday she ran out. The baby was hungry because her mother couldn't produce milk."

"I don't see what this has to do with me," Kyle responded, although he had an uncomfortable suspicion that in Mark's mind, somehow the woman had become his responsibility.

"We've talked about your work on many occasions," Mark said.

"Argued about my work, you mean," Kyle corrected. "You preaching, me defending."

"You've done some preaching yourself. A lot of preaching about being fair, and about your job being to see that justice is served."

"I'll be damned," Kyle remarked. "You were actually listening."

"If ever there's been a case where justice needed serving, it's with that woman in the kitchen."

"Ah, yes. The nursing mother and her baby. I can see where the Madonna aspect would appeal to your sense of drama."

"That statement isn't worthy of you, Kyle."

Kyle dismissed the admonition and picked up his beer.

"The baby's father won't have anything to do with her, or the baby," Mark said.

"He must be a real winner."

"It's your kind of case," Mark pointed out. "You could bring him to heel if anyone can."

"Bring him to heel?" Kyle repeated incredulously. "Father Darby, that sounded almost vindictive. You wouldn't stoop to revenge, would you?"

"Revenge . . . Justice . . . It's a matter of semantics. If you're asking if I'd like to see the man forced to live up to his responsibilities, then, yes, I'd stoop to that. And you're going to help me."

"You ask a lot in the name of friendship," Kyle muttered. "Preparation time alone on a case like that would run into the thousands."

"If you weren't taking it on *pro bono publico*."

"For the public good," Kyle translated wryly.

Mark scowled at his sarcasm. "To my way of seeing it, it could be for Kyle Sawyer Brooks's good, most of all."

"Still trying to save me from my greedy, avaricious ways?"

"Giving you the opportunity to save yourself," Mark said.

"What makes you so sure I'll take it on?"

"Because I'm asking you to."

"It's been a long time since we were best friends."

"That's not my doing," Mark said, pinning Kyle with a hard look that made Kyle shift in his chair. "You'll take the case because you're an honorable man."

Again, Kyle sniffed his disdain at the suggestion.

"You don't owe me, Kyle," Mark pressed, "but you think you do. Your honor, no matter how misguided, won't let you refuse. And we both know why."

Kyle set his empty beer can on Mark's desk with a thunk.

"The guilt is consuming you. It's been eating at you ever since—" An expression of gut-wrenching pain contorted Kyle's face. "I've been watching you for years, Kyle, blaming yourself, punishing yourself. Here's your chance to work off some of that guilt."

"What good—?"

"You want atonement? Here's your chance." The urgency of conviction entered his voice. "Nothing you can do will bring Shannon back, Kyle. You can wallow in guilt, you can let it form a hard crust around your heart, but that won't change the fact that Shannon's dead."

Kyle glared at him. "So, what am I doing here?"

"That woman in my kitchen," Mark continued, pointing for emphasis, "*is* alive, and she needs help. I can give her a bowl of soup, but that's only a stopgap measure. You're uniquely qualified to give her the kind of help that'll make a difference."

"You just won't give it a rest, will you?" Kyle complained.

"I've never seen two people who needed each other more," Mark replied.

"That's rich. Now I need this woman?"

"You need to believe in your own basic goodness again," Mark explained softly.

"About as much as I need to believe in Santa Claus and the tooth fairy," Kyle grumbled. "Don't talk to me in priest gibberish, Mark. We go too far back for that."

There was a strained silence as their eyes locked.

"All right," Mark said, throwing his hands in the air. "No priest gibberish, no pressure. I'm asking for your help, friend to friend. The choice is yours. Help me or walk out. No hard feelings, either way."

Another silence.

"Damn you!" Kyle said finally.

Mark cracked a smile. "Why don't we leave that matter to a Higher Authority."

"I'll take the case, okay?" Kyle said, irritated at Mark for having manipulated him.

Mark nodded, acknowledging his victory. "Now, let me tell you how this is going to work. Is that housekeeping post at your house still open?"

"Oh, no." Kyle shook his head. *Mark couldn't be serious!* "I agreed to take the case. I need two *pro bono* cases a year to stay square with the Orange County Bar Association. I can probably use some of the prep time as a tax write-off. I'll represent her, but you're not going to saddle me with some down-and-out case with a baby. Do-gooding is your thing, not mine."

"She needs a place to stay."

"There's no vacancy at my place."

"That's not what you were saying a couple of weeks ago, when you were giving my mother that sob story about needing someone to organize that fancy new house of yours—the one with the maid's quarters off the kitchen."

"I need a housekeeper, not a charity case."

"Meredith needs a chance, not charity."

"No. Absolutely not."

"She can do the job, Kyle. She was three years into a degree in home economics before she had to drop out of college."

"I'm not turning my home into a halfway house."

"She wants to work. She was a waitress until she had some health problems during her pregnancy. That's when she got in trouble financially. It wasn't a nice, cushy job with maternity benefits."

"You're breaking my heart."

"I'm glad to hear you still have a heart to break," Mark said sharply. "Sometimes I've wondered."

"Don't make me out to be the bad guy in this scenario," Kyle replied. "I didn't create her problems. And just because I don't want to get involved—"

"She wants to work," Mark repeated. "You need a housekeeper. She's got three years of college to back up her credentials."

"She's got a baby."

"That's why she's not working. She has no one to baby-sit. The baby's just weeks old, much too young for day care. They wouldn't even let her work at a child-care center until the baby is three months old."

"Strike up the violins for background music for this sob story," Kyle quipped sarcastically.

"You said you couldn't find time to interview house-keepers. Well, I'm dropping one in your lap. Pay her a salary—enough to take care of herself and the baby—and give her a little dignity. Withhold a percentage in exchange for your legal fees if you want. Make her feel a little less like a charity case."

"What do you know about this woman?" Kyle asked. "How do you know that anything she's told you is true?"

"You met her."

"Oh, she's down-and-out, all right. But that doesn't make her honest."

"I'd stake my life that everything she's told me is the absolute truth."

"You're a priest," Kyle said. "Faith and trust are your jurisdiction. I'm an attorney. Skepticism is mine. She could have me cleaned out in a week's time."

"I'll take complete responsibility," Mark declared.

Kyle laughed. "If she waltzes off with the silver, I'm supposed to come to you for compensation? How would you repay me—blood from a turnip? Water from stone?" He paused before asking, "Why did you drag me into this?"

"I was betting on the fact that you have enough human compassion left to help out a fellow human being, especially when it works to your benefit."

Kyle spit out a blistering expletive.

"Fifty Hail Marys," Mark pronounced dryly.

A long silence followed, then Mark continued somberly, "I don't want to feed her into the system, Kyle. She's been living in her car, but so far she hasn't been out on the streets. If we send her out to the 'proper authorities,' that's where she'll end up. She doesn't belong there, any more than Shannon would have."

"Quit using emotional blackmail on me. Shannon has no place in this discussion."

"All right. No more cheap tricks. Just a straightforward request. Help this woman, Kyle. Help her because she's a human being in need and you're a human being with human kindness to give."

After hesitating, Kyle said, "You know you're the one person I can't turn down."

"Uh-uh," Mark parried. "I let you off the hook, remember? It's your decision. I'm just urging you to do the right thing."

Kyle repeated the same expletive. This time Mark assigned no Hail Marys, even in jest; he was too busy savoring his victory.

2

"I'M NOT GOING TO steal you blind." It was probably a dumb thing to say, but Meredith felt she had to say something. The silence in the sedan had grown oppressive. The owner of the car, as sleek and elegant as his vehicle, turned his head to look at her directly. It was the first time she'd felt she truly had his attention.

"I'm destitute, but I'm no thief," she said.

"I wasn't—"

"I don't blame you. I'd be suspicious in your place." Suddenly unable to deal with the intimacy of their face-to-face confrontation, she turned away, dropping her gaze first to her lap, then lifting it again to the scenery sliding past the window on her right.

He didn't answer her, which gave her the opportunity to reflect on what she'd just said. In his place, she *would* be suspicious. Obviously this man—she strained to remember his name and couldn't—had a lot to lose. The priest had said his house had maid's quarters, and maid's quarters were hardly standard equipment in your typical three-bedroom suburban house.

She rested the side of her head against the car window. The glass was cool, rather like a moist cloth against her brow. She'd seldom had anything to lose, and she'd always been wary of strangers. Maybe deprivation made a person more wary. Maybe having less made you more possessive of what you did have, more afraid of losing it.

She exhaled heavily, fogging the glass. Why was he doing it? Why was he taking in a homeless woman and a baby? Of the possible reasons that came to mind, old-fashioned Christian charity seemed the least likely of all. He was too tense, too remote. *Too cool.*

He wasn't the expansive, generous type who made spontaneous gestures out of the goodness of his heart. She had the distinct impression he'd rather be driving to check himself into a medieval torture chamber for a few hours on the rack than driving her to his house. It was the priest's doing; she was sure of it. The priest had called him in and coerced him into taking her on as a housekeeper.

She wondered briefly what type of leverage the priest might have used. Appearances could be deceiving, of course, but Mr. Cool didn't seem the type who could be pressured easily. He was too . . .

Meredith groped for a suitable word but couldn't find one. Her mind was dulled by fatigue. She was tired, exhausted, worn-out. At a time when she'd needed rest to regain her strength, she'd been sleeping scrunched in the back seat of her compact car, unable to stretch out fully, unable to get comfortable; unable to sleep well when she did drop off because of buzzing insects and blaring lights and the highway sounds of whirring engines, screaming brakes and honking horns.

Priest or no priest, she should be as wary of going into a strange man's house as Mr. Cool was of taking a stranger under his roof. But after knowing fear—fear so intense she could literally taste it in her mouth—*wary* was hardly worth the energy. She'd been afraid of burly truck drivers, of grungy-looking motorcyclists, of men who stared at her in a way that made her feel sullied and ashamed. She'd feared being murdered in her sleep, or being raped and beaten, and having her daughter kidnapped. She'd feared starving to death or contracting diseases in dirty bathrooms. She'd feared growing too weak or getting too ill to protect her daughter.

Going into the home of a stranger recommended by a priest was nothing at all to fear after what she'd been through. There would be a roof and a real bed and peace—and tomorrow there would be food for breakfast.

KYLE STARED at the door on the passenger side of his car, wondering what to do about the woman sleeping with her head braced against the window. He'd hoped she'd wake up when the engine stopped, or later, when he slammed the door on the driver's side after getting out of the car. Now he debated between getting back into the car and trying to wake her, or opening the door.

He opted for opening the door. With the seat belt fastened she was not in imminent danger of tumbling out; perhaps she'd stir when the window gave way beneath her head.

Kyle didn't want to have to shake her awake. He didn't want to touch her at all. The situation Mark had placed him in was awkward enough without giving her any opportunity to try to pin him with accusations of physical advances. If the lady—and he used the term loosely, considering the appearance of the woman— was of a devious mind, she would figure out soon enough that the best angle to work would be improper conduct on his behalf.

Kyle suddenly realized how vulnerable he was. Had Mark given *that* any thought when he'd sent a woman home with him? Surely Mark hadn't forgotten about sex just because he'd become a priest and taken a vow of chastity.

Well, he wasn't going to give Little Miss Down-and-Out any ammunition to use against him—not that she presented any temptation. Gaunt women with haunted eyes were not his type. He'd never been afflicted with the urge to protect women who didn't have the good sense or initiative to take care of themselves.

She jerked awake with a shrill gasp when he opened the door. "Stacy?" Panicking, she twisted against the seat belt until she could see her baby, who was sleeping soundly in the infant carrier strapped to the center of the rear car seat.

"She's fine," Kyle said. "I'm sorry I had to wake you, but we're here."

"It's all right," Meredith answered woozily. Moving slowly, as though infirm, she pulled herself out of the car and opened the back door so she could take the baby, infant seat and all.

"I can get that bag," Kyle offered as she moved to slide the strap over her shoulder.

"Thank you," she acknowledged softly, without letting her eyes meet his.

The bag was heavier than he'd anticipated, and Kyle wondered how she'd managed to lug it and the infant seat around.

They entered the house through the side door, directly into the kitchen. Kyle walked to an interior door on the far wall and opened it. "This is the maid's quarters. It's empty now, but you can shop for the basics when you feel up to it. A bed, chest of drawers, maybe a picture or two—whatever you and the baby need. Until we get these quarters set up you can stay in the guest room. I'll show you where it is."

He flicked on the light in the first bedroom off the hall. "This is it."

He experienced a moment of unease as she looked around the room, absorbing it. It was a nice room, he supposed, trying to visualize it through her eyes. He wasn't much for decorating, but he'd found a helpful salesclerk at the furniture store and bought the bedspread and pictures when he'd bought the bedroom suite, and he knew the room was passably attractive.

"There are towels in the bathroom," he went on. "Just forage for anything—"

"A real shower!" The words gushed forth like a passionate proclamation.

Kyle felt a brush of panic at the expression in her eyes. She was going to cry. He was well acquainted with women's tears and recognized the foreshadowing symptoms. The women he represented always cried, even the ones who came in fueled by hard anger. Eventually even they cried, because anything that had the power to provoke anger also had the power to draw tears of bitterness and pain.

He could deal with it at the office. He kept a box of tissues in his desk drawer and terry washcloths at the wet bar so the women could blot their noses and repair their makeup before leaving. His home was a different matter. He didn't need a hysterical woman in his home. Home was his haven, and he didn't want to have to produce tissues or cool compresses on demand.

"There are some toiletries in a basket," he told her, anxious to escape before her tears erupted. "Just help yourself."

"My toothbrush and shampoo are in my car."

"Mark—Father Mark—had your car towed to a garage owned by one of his flock. He's going to see if we can get it brought here when the tire is repaired. In the meantime, help yourself to anything in the basket."

She nodded.

"If there's anything else you need, tonight or tomorrow while I'm at the office—"

"I could use your washer and dryer, if that's okay." Again there was that rush of emotion in her voice.

"Sure," Kyle replied. "Whatever. We'll . . . uh, discuss the terms of your employment tomorrow evening."

Her chin quivered as she nodded again, and Kyle felt another wave of panic. The flight response rose in full force. He had to get out of this room, away from the onslaught of hysteria. He could give the woman a job, even legal representation, but he'd be damned if he was going to be stuck shoving tissues under the nose of a *pro bono* case.

"Good night," he said abruptly and made his escape.

Meredith mumbled a good-night to his retreating figure and forced herself to wait a polite moment before closing the door. Eyes closed, she leaned against it and sighed. Space. Safe, private space within four walls and under a roof. How long had it been since she'd felt security and privacy? It seemed an eternity. She shivered with the intense feeling of relief. No more whining engines, squealing brakes or blaring horns. No more glaring lights. No more truck drivers with biceps the size of hams or seedy bikers or weirdos. No more open air bathrooms with concrete floors.

Her own *bathroom*. The thought gave her enough energy to peel herself away from the door and walk to the bathroom. Vinyl flooring in a muted, tasteful pattern. Velour towels. Scented soap balls. Bath mat an inch thick. A shower stall with tile floor and walls visible through the etched-glass door. The tears she'd been keeping in check could be held back no longer. She stood in the middle of the room and cried at the beauty of ordinary things she'd always taken for granted.

She dropped to the floor, braced her elbows on her bent knees and buried her face in her hands, while her shoulders vibrated with the force of her sobs. She couldn't have said how long she sat there, her bottom on the smooth floor, shedding tears of joy and relief and utter despondency.

Stacy's cry drew her back into the world. She ripped a length of toilet paper from the dispenser near her head and wiped her nose with it. Then, with a burst of enthusiasm, she went to her daughter and unstrapped her from the infant seat.

"Poor baby. Poor Stacy. Did you wake up somewhere strange and not see Mommy? You're not hungry again, are you?"

Stacy stopped crying when Meredith lifted her from the infant seat. "No, I didn't think so. Not hungry yet. You had a full bottle of formula, didn't you?"

The priest had called on a parishioner to go to the store for formula and a bottle and disposable diapers and bring them to the rectory. "Yeah. Mommy's well had run dry." *But only temporarily,* she thought fiercely. Now that she would be eating regularly, she would produce enough milk.

"I'll feed you later, sweetheart," she told Stacy, touching her nose as she smiled down at her. "Right now, we're going to take a shower. A real shower. With all the warm water we want, and wonderful soap."

Reaching into the diaper bag, she found the liquid baby soap that had come in the baby-care kit at the hospital. "Guess I'll have the fancy soap, and you'll have the usual. Don't fret, though. We're going to have nice, thick, clean towels. Come on, let's get this gown off, and your diaper. Ooo, Stacy, no wonder you were fussing. You needed a change, didn't you? We'll put on a fresh one after your shower, and a fresh shirt and, guess what? Tomorrow we're going to wash all your clothes properly. No more cold water in dirty sinks. We're going to throw them in a real washing machine."

Meredith undressed and hung her clothing on the towel rack. Cradling her naked daughter in the crook of her left arm, she sifted through the basket of toiletries, picking out what she needed before turning on the water and adjusting it. Stacy fretted a little when she first stepped under the warm spray, then stilled as Meredith spoke reassuringly to her and slathered soap over her tiny body. When Stacy was thoroughly rinsed, Meredith carried her out of the stall and blotted her dry, then wrapped her loosely in the towel and centered her on the thick bath mat.

"If you need anything, just cry out, sweetheart," she said before getting back into the shower. This time she let the water run hotter, and sighed at the sensation of it spraying through her hair. She breathed in the herbal scent of the shampoo from the basket as she lathered her hair, thinking that she would wash her hair every day for the rest of her life if she could have access to a clean, private bathroom and hot water.

The conditioner was as rich as the shampoo. Meredith left it in her hair while she spread shower gel over her body.

Her breasts felt heavy, and Meredith marveled at the miracle that enabled a woman's body to produce milk. *Just wait, Stacy. Wait until I've eaten three square meals a day for a few days. You're going to be the best-fed baby in town!*

She shaved her legs. How feminine it seemed, performing that simple ritual! It made her feel—civilized. Yes. That was it. Civilized. As though by shaving her legs she'd moved from the netherworld of the homeless back into civilized society.

The shower stall filled with fragrant steam as she rinsed the conditioner from her hair. If there is a heaven, she thought, it would smell and feel like this. Or perhaps heaven was a thick, soft towel to wrap up in, she amended seconds later, as she dried herself. She should have satin or lace—or cotton batiste at the very least—to wear after such an experience, she decided; but she had to settle for the stretched-out T-shirt she'd been wearing all day, because her clothes were in her car. There was little lace or batiste in her wardrobe, anyway. T-shirts were more economical, and economy had been a necessity for as long as she could remember.

After putting a diaper and shirt on Stacy, Meredith placed her in the seat and moved it next to the bed, where she would be able to reach her if she fretted during the night. Stacy was sound asleep by the time Meredith had rinsed out her own underwear and hung it in the shower stall to dry.

When at last Meredith folded back the bedspread, she gasped at the beauty of the sheets. They were edged in lace and had flowers on them. Who would have thought Mr. Cool would have flowered sheets?

She slid her hands over them almost reverently, enjoying the smoothness of them. Percale. How long had it been since she'd slept on percale sheets? It had been over a week since she'd slept on any sheets at all.

The nightlight in the bathroom cast a muted glow into the bedroom, and the sheets felt deliciously cool as she crawled between them and stretched her body full length over the mattress. They smelled clean, with a hint of fabric softener—a welcome contrast to the slightly fuelish odor that clung to the back seat of her car.

Meredith dropped her arm over the side of the bed to caress Stacy's cheek with her fingertips before raising it again to plump the pillow under her own cheek. She felt tears gathering in her eyes but closed her lids against them.

Within minutes, she was asleep.

Within an hour, Stacy was awake and howling. Meredith lifted her into the bed, tucked her under the covers next to her and nursed her. "This is a bed," she whispered as Stacy suckled her right breast. "A real bed. One day you'll have a bed like this. But first, we're going to get you a crib. I know. You don't know what that is, but you're going to find out. Father Mark is going to see if any of his parishioners have one sitting around gathering dust."

She shifted the baby to her other breast. "If Father Mark says he'll find us a crib, he'll find us a crib. He's already found me a job so we'll have a place to live. I'd say he's a miracle worker, wouldn't you?"

Meredith sighed. "Soon you'll have a real crib, and we'll clean it up and put clean sheets with bunny rabbits on them in it, and you'll forget all about living in the car."

She laughed softly. "Now, that'll be a real miracle, won't it? And we're not even Catholic!"

3

KYLE DIALED HIS HOME number, then beat an impatient tattoo on his desk with a pencil eraser as he listened to his own voice telling him he wasn't home and inviting him to leave a message. His grip on the receiver tightened as he heard the beep. "Meredith! If you're listening, if you can hear me, pick up the phone. This is Kyle. I forgot to turn off the answering machine, but I need to talk to you."

After a full minute of dead silence he hung up, cursing under his breath. Let yourself be talked into a good deed and all you got for your trouble was aggravation! If he couldn't get his so-called housekeeper on the phone soon, he was going to have to swing by home on his lunch hour—assuming he still had a home. Hopefully she hadn't found a way to pack up his house and cart it off with her when she left.

If she were there, surely she would have picked up the phone by now. She couldn't be so dense that she didn't understand telephone answering machines, and since his was on the built-in desk in the kitchen, she most certainly would have heard his frantic appeals for her to pick up the phone. Wasn't it logical that she would have been in the kitchen at some point when he called? Everybody had to eat.

Recalling the note he'd left on the butcher-block island in the kitchen, he nodded. She'd been to the kitchen, all right. Been there, grabbed the note and absconded with the grocery money, most likely. He must have been temporarily insane to let Mark intimidate him into taking in a total stranger off the street.

Tilting his head back over the rim of the back of his chair, Kyle sighed resignedly. If Mark's desperate Madonna had run off with the money from the cookie jar, at least she was no longer his problem; and no one, not even Mark, could say Kyle hadn't tried to help her. Some people just couldn't be helped, and this woman had Loser written all over her.

MEREDITH GENTLY EASED her sleeping daughter into the infant seat. She'd nursed her once during the night and again upon awakening, and now it was time to see about some nourishment for herself. Yawning, she stretched, thinking how wonderful it was to have slept in a bed again after all the mornings of waking up with painful kinks from being scrunched in the back seat of her car.

The clock on the bedside table told her it was almost ten-thirty. Lord, when was the last time she'd slept until ten, and lain in bed till ten-thirty?

Meredith's gaze dropped to her sleeping daughter. Had Stacy somehow sensed her mother's exhaustion, and sudden absence of fear that had allowed her to sleep soundly and securely? Is that why Stacy had slept until ten o'clock?

Meredith dropped onto the side of the bed, buried her face in her hands and groaned. What kind of messages had she been sending to her baby daughter? She'd tried so hard to protect Stacy, to make her feel safe, when she herself had been consumed by anxiety. Had the tension in her body undermined her conscious effort to shield her daughter?

Meredith's hands fell into her lap. Looking at Stacy's tranquil face, she squared her shoulders in resolve— *No more. Never again, little one.*

With that decision made, she carried the infant seat to the kitchen and positioned it in the center of the butcher-block island. Spying an envelope sticking out from under the bottom of the seat, she tilted the seat up and pulled the envelope out. It had her name on it in block letters.

She stared at it for several seconds. The envelope was of a quality paper stock, starkly white, with a security lining. A return address was printed in the upper left corner. Kyle Sawyer Brooks. The flap was sealed. How like a man like Mr. Cool to seal an envelope he wasn't even mailing! She tore open the envelope. *Money!* Twenty-dollar bills, five of them clipped neatly together with a paper clip. Her fingers trembled as she counted them. Was he testing her? Paying her off? Asking her to leave and appeasing his conscience with cash?

She breathed easier when she found a note inside the envelope.

Meredith,
If you get your car today, you might want to start stocking the pantry. This should cover a few basics and anything you or the baby need until we can work out a household budget.

He'd signed his full name—first, middle, last: "Kyle Sawyer Brooks." Meredith crammed the note and the money back into the envelope, tossed it on the table and walked over to the refrigerator. Finding a carton of orange juice, she poured herself a glass and sipped it as she scanned the shelves of the walk-in pantry to check out the food supply. Sugar, coffee creamer, mixed nuts, some sesame crackers, high-fiber breakfast cereal, several cans of water-packed tuna. At least she'd have lunch—she remembered seeing mayonnaise and gherkins in the refrigerator.

She took a tin of tuna from the pantry, searched for a can opener, and finally found one in a storage niche built into the side of the island. The phone rang. She debated whether to answer it when Kyle's voice startled her.

An answering machine! She should have guessed that Mr. Cool would have an answering machine.

"Wait for the tone," Kyle Sawyer Brooks's voice ordered.

"Wait for the tone," Meredith parroted, mimicking his arrogant manner of speaking. Instantly she felt guilty about her petty behavior, reminding herself whose house she was in and in whose guest bed she had slept. Whether she liked Mr. Kyle Sawyer Brooks or not, she was out of her car and off the streets because of the job he'd given her.

The shrill tone sounded and woke Stacy, and she wailed. Meredith dashed to the infant seat and started undoing the straps so she could pick her up and comfort her.

"Meredith, if you're listening, please pick up the phone."

Meredith looked from her crying baby to the telephone and back and frantically hurried with the straps so she could carry Stacy with her to answer it.

"I've been trying to call you all morning. I have an important message. Please, if you can hear my voice—"

Meredith finally managed to get Stacy out of the seat and dashed across the room to pick up the phone. "Hello?"

"Meredith?"

He sounded so shocked she was tempted to say something smart, like "No, it's the Easter Bunny." But she controlled the impulse. He was her employer, and this post as housekeeper was the most important job she'd ever held. "Yes, Mr. Brooks," she said, struggling to sound professional while Stacy was hollering her head off less than a foot away from the receiver.

"Your baby is crying."

"The beep woke her up. I'm trying to calm her down."

"She's all right, isn't she?"

"She's just startled." Meredith jiggled her shoulder up and down, trying to quiet Stacy with the familiar motion.

"Can you hear me?" she heard Mr. Brooks ask impatiently.

"Yes." By wedging the phone between her ear and her shoulder, she was able to free her hand to pat Stacy's back. Stacy's screams subsided into a gurgle and then a string of isolated snuffles.

"Thank goodness," Kyle said into the resultant silence. "I don't know how anyone could concentrate with all that noise."

"Focus," Meredith replied.

A skeptical harrumph came over the line.

"I think it's a special ability that comes with giving birth."

Ignoring the comment, Kyle went on, "I've been trying to call you all morning."

"I thought I heard the phone a little while ago, but it quit ringing after the first ring."

"It's that damned machine. We're going to have to take it off immediate ring." He gave her instructions and she switched the button so that the machine would answer after five rings. It was no small task, with a phone receiver tucked against one shoulder and Stacy nestled against the other.

"Mark—Father Mark—called this morning to say that the mechanic who towed your car will come by for you around one. The man's name is Jerry. Mark wanted me to talk to you and let you know it's okay to go with him. He was afraid you might be nervous about leaving with a stranger."

He spoke the last sentence as though the concept of a woman being wary of strangers was incredible to him. Perhaps Meredith thought, it was incredible to him that a woman who'd been "homeless" and "destitute" would have any qualms left about *anything*.

Undaunted, Kyle continued. "Mark said something about taking you to a thrift shop the church maintains to see if there's anything you or the baby could use. Then he'll take you to the garage for your car."

"I'll be ready." After a brief silence she added, "I found the note and the grocery money."

"Good. If you need to shop—"

"Actually, I was more concerned about the car. If I could pay for the repairs out of the money you left, then we could deduct it from my first month's salary."

"I've already made arrangements about the car."

"I—" Meredith began, but couldn't complete the thought.

"You'll be needing it for shopping and errands," Kyle went on. "I don't think a car allowance would be out of line."

"Thank you," she said in a near whisper. Another silence ensued before she asked, "Is there anything specific you'd like for dinner?"

"Dinner?" He made it sound as though it were an abstract idea.

"Since I'll be shopping, I thought—"

"Don't you want to take a few days to get settled before you start cooking?"

"I'll have to cook for myself. It's no more trouble for two."

"Whatever. Actually, I thought tonight might be a good time to get some preliminary information about your suit."

It was Meredith's turn to sound blank. "Suit?"

"You're planning on suing the child's father for support, aren't you? I thought that's why Mark called me instead of one of his parishioners."

"I guess," Meredith replied.

"You sound ambivalent."

"It's not...easy," she said, and paused. "It's an...awkward situation."

"Becoming destitute because you don't demand help is awkward," Kyle told her. "Not demanding help is stupid."

A long silence stretched over the line. "We'll talk about it tonight," he said finally. "And Meredith..."

"Yes?"

"About dinner...I'm not a fussy eater. Anything'll do."

"What time do you usually get home?"

"It varies." Then, as though reconsidering, he amended, "Six-thirty. I'll be home at six-thirty this evening. That should give us time to go over the general information."

There was another extended silence. "Mr. Brooks?"

"Yes?"

"Thank you. For everything."

Kyle cleared his throat. "I have an appointment in a few minutes."

Meredith hung up the phone and gave Stacy a hug. "Our new boss isn't so bad. He may not be Mr. Congeniality, but we can live with that, can't we?" Without giving voice to the words, she thought, *To keep a roof over our heads, we can live with a lot.*

KYLE WASN'T LOOKING forward to a face-to-face encounter with his new housekeeper. He wondered *how* he'd let Mark talk him into this idiotic situation. Although he'd mentioned needing a housekeeper in passing, he'd been in no hurry to hire one. In fact, he'd been on the verge of signing a contract for a once-a-week housekeeping service that would probably have been more than adequate for his needs ninety percent of the time. The other ten percent of the time he could hire caterers.

A housekeeping service wouldn't have him racing home at a certain hour for dinner. Outside his work, he didn't like being accountable to anyone, and he wasn't going to let a hired housekeeper install any time clocks in his own home—even figurative ones. That was something he was going to clear up when they discussed the terms of her employment. He worked late when he felt like working late, went home when it pleased him to go home, ate out when the mood hit him, and he wasn't about to change his life-style for the hired help—especially when he'd been coerced into hiring the help.

A battered compact car was parked at the curb in front of his house. The housekeeper's, no doubt. Obviously she'd made it home from the mechanic's shop. As he turned into the drive, he realized that he was going to have to instruct her to park her car on the driveway near the double garage and assign her a side. The community association would be sending him nasty letters reminding him of the deed restrictions regarding cars parked at the curb if he didn't.

He entered the house through the side door. The air in the kitchen was full of the scent of cooking food, but his new housekeeper was nowhere in sight. Kyle heaved a sigh of something that might have been relief over not having to face her the moment he walked in the door.

Habit took him to his desk, where he deposited his briefcase and checked the answering machine. The only messages were the ones he'd left for Meredith early in the day. He erased them, then wandered over to the stove and lifted the lid on the Dutch oven with his right hand. His suit coat was hooked over the fingers of his left hand.

"It's beef stew," explained a voice behind him.

Kyle dropped the lid and turned. Meredith walked toward him from the direction of the laundry room. "It smells good," he said.

"There's salad, too. I can serve dinner anytime you're ready."

Kyle lifted his left hand to jiggle the coat meaningfully. "I'd like to get comfortable first."

She nodded. "I'll start heating the bread."

Kyle turned to leave, then stopped to look at her again. "Where's your baby?"

"Sleeping."

It was the first time he'd seen her smile, and it took him aback slightly to notice that she was wearing lipstick. She'd done something to her hair, too. *Probably washed it*, he thought snidely.

"Father Mark rustled up a crib," she continued. "Jerry brought it over. It's the first time Stacy's had a proper bed."

Eyes averted, she hesitated, as though considering broaching a dreaded subject. Kyle tensed, wondering what she was going to bring up.

"I set it up in the room you said would be my quarters. I thought that would be easier than putting it in the guest room and having to move it later."

"That sounds logical," Kyle said, relieved that the issue was an insignificant one.

"I'll be able to hear her when I'm working during the day," Meredith continued. "Of course, at night, I'll want her in the guest room with me. I found a portable bassinet at the thrift shop. She'll be fine in it for a few nights."

Kyle nodded. There seemed to be no end to the complications a baby presented, which made him glad he was a man with a housekeeper with a baby instead of a man with a wife and child.

"There was a bed at the thrift shop," Meredith went on. "Head- and footboards and rails. It's pretty battered, but it's solid wood, so I thought—if it was all right with you—that I could paint it and put it in my quarters."

"You don't have to do that," Kyle told her. "You can buy whatever—"

"I don't mind," Meredith said. "I like working with old furniture. It's usually constructed better than what they make nowadays."

Kyle shrugged. "Paint it, then. You can get a mattress and box spring when you're shopping for the other furnishings."

"It'll be attractive," Meredith assured him.

"I'm sure it will," Kyle responded, thinking he couldn't care less what it looked like if they could just quit discussing it to death. He shifted the coat slung over his shoulder and exhaled heavily. "I'm going to get comfortable."

Meredith put two rolls in the oven and carried the salad and a glass of ice water to the place she'd set for Kyle in the formal dining room. She stirred the stew and ran hot water into the serving bowl to warm it, then waited for Kyle in the dining room.

He was back in a few minutes wearing a polo-type shirt tucked neatly into cotton slacks, and loafers without socks. Eyeing the single place setting, he asked, "Aren't you eating?"

"I ate earlier," she said. "I didn't think you'd want—"

"Oh."

"Would you like iced tea or milk?"

"Water's fine."

Meredith nodded and scurried into the kitchen for his food. He was eating his salad when she returned with the stew and the rolls, which she'd wrapped in a linen napkin and put in a small breadbasket.

"Is that salad dressing all right? It was the only kind in the refrigerator, so I assumed you liked it."

"It's fine," he answered brusquely.

"I'll be in the kitchen if you need anything."

"There's no bell," Kyle commented wryly.

"The kitchen's only ten feet away," Meredith pointed out. "Whistle. You know how to whistle, don't you?"

The plucky humor was unexpected. "I saw the movie on the late, late show," he replied. "You just put your lips together and blow, right?"

"Close enough," Meredith said, and left the room. In the kitchen she ladled the leftover stew into a storage bowl and filled the Dutch oven with warm soapy water. She'd just begun scrubbing when she heard movement behind her. Turning, she discovered Kyle settling at the small table in the breakfast nook, arranging his plate, glass and flatware appropriately in front of him. "Have a seat," he told her, indicating the chair opposite him.

Meredith hesitated, but when his gaze fixed with hers and his eyes narrowed into an I-gave-an-order expression, she rinsed and dried her hands and went to the table as requested.

He put down his fork and sighed dismally. "We have to talk," he said, with all the enthusiasm of a doctor about to tell a favorite patient he was terminally ill.

Meredith panicked. What if he told her he'd reconsidered, that he didn't need a housekeeper? She and Stacy would be out on the road again, and Stacy wouldn't have a crib.

"I understand what you're trying to do," Kyle told her, in the tone he would use with a child. "The formal dining room, eating separately. But it's not going to work."

Meredith forced herself to stay calm and think positive thoughts. Father Mark would help them again. *Someone* would help them. She *couldn't* go back to living in the car. She *wouldn't*.

He paused, searching for the right way to express himself. "Look, I mentioned to Mark that I needed a housekeeper, but I don't need— I'm not a formal person in my own home. What I'm trying to say is, I never eat in the dining room unless I have guests. The kitchen is fine."

"I just wanted—"

"I know. And I appreciate it. But I'm not an ogre. And this isn't a manor in eighteenth-century England. You don't have to be so . . . formal."

"I'll try not to be," she replied.

That seemed to please him. "Another thing," he went on. "I don't always— My schedule tends to be erratic. Sometimes I come home, grab a bite and go out for the evening, and sometimes I go out to dinner straight from the office, or go out somewhere and then come home and slap together a sandwich."

"Tuna," Meredith said.

"Whatever's available," Kyle said. "The point is, I don't come home for dinner at the same time every night, and some nights I don't come home for dinner at all."

"All right."

"All right?"

"All right," Meredith repeated. "Obviously you don't want a rigid dinner schedule."

"No. I don't."

Meredith shrugged. "Then I'll make sure there are groceries around and try to keep some heatables in the refrigerator."

"'Heatables'?"

"You know, something that can be heated up on the spur of the moment. Like this stew. Or something that can be frozen in single-meal quantities."

Kyle pondered what she'd said for several seconds. "That sounds reasonable. Yes, I think that'll work nicely. This stew is very good, by the way." He took a bite for emphasis.

Meredith acknowledged the compliment with a small nod. After all the peanut butter she'd eaten, beef stew had been like nectar from the gods. "Are you a meat-and-potatoes eater?" she asked.

"I'm not picky."

"It would be helpful if you'd make a list of some of the things you like to eat."

"I told you, I'm not picky."

"If I knew what foods you like, I'd know how to shop."

"I like simple foods, okay? What I don't like is to make a federal case out of food."

Ex-cuse me, Meredith thought. She'd just have to use the dartboard approach until she discovered what his tastes were. So be it. It was his grocery money—and his stomach. She was just happy to be facing the prospect of regular meals. Her tongue tingled with the urge to tell him exactly that, but she resisted. If she wanted regular meals, she needed the job this man was providing.

Stacy saved her from having to reply at all, with a whimper followed by a swelling cry. Meredith leaped up and gave Kyle an apologetic shrug. "She's been asleep for hours. I'm sure she's hungry. I'll have to feed her."

Stacy was crying in earnest now, punctuating hefty wails with angry screams.

"Do what you have to do," Kyle said.

Meredith went to Stacy and picked her up, bouncing her on her shoulder in a futile effort to soothe her.

She paused in the kitchen on the way to the guest room where she would breast-feed the baby in privacy.

"She's definitely hungry," she told Kyle. "Leave the dishes and I'll clear them away after she's fed."

After Stacy had nursed, Meredith bathed her. "Now you'll smell nice," she said, massaging a dab of baby lotion into the baby's skin. She'd been using the trial-size bottle of lotion from the hospital take-home kit sparingly, but she was down to the last few drops. She'd have to remember to put lotion on the grocery list.

Closing her eyes, she shuddered. The list of what she and Stacy needed seemed endless; baby lotion seemed so superfluous after what they'd been through, yet— was it so unreasonable to want to be able to smooth lotion over her baby's skin?

She opened her eyes and smiled down at Stacy's sweet face. "You like the way it feels when I rub your little feet, don't you? Well, there's nothing extravagant about making you feel good, little lady. Don't ever let anyone tell you different."

Lifting a gown from the stack of laundry she'd done that morning, Meredith continued, "Guess what we've got. Clean clothes. Really clean, and soft. Oh, and you're so pretty in your clean clothes."

She scooped Stacy into her arms. "Come on, sweetheart. Your infant seat is in the other room. We'll put you in it, and you can watch Mommy wash dishes."

Kyle was watching the evening news on television. As she passed through the living room en route to the kitchen, he hit the remote control switch to turn off the television and stood. "Ready to discuss business?"

Meredith stopped to look at him as she spoke. "I was going to finish up in the kitchen."

"The kitchen can wait," Kyle told her. "I'd like to get some preliminary information for the suit."

"All right," Meredith said, her reluctance obvious.

Meredith took a seat at the dining-room table with Stacy in her lap and watched Kyle take a tape recorder and yellow legal pad from his briefcase.

"I didn't think they were using those anymore," she remarked.

"Does it make you nervous?" he asked, touching the recorder.

"I meant the yellow pad. I read somewhere that yellow paper isn't recyclable, so the legal community was switching to white legal pads."

The expression on Kyle's face betrayed impatience. "If that's true, the news hasn't filtered down to Orlando in a big way. I'll check into it. If there's anything to it, I'll have my office manager order white from now on." He drummed his fingers on the table next to the recorder, then moved his hand to the controls. "Ready?"

Meredith instinctively hugged Stacy tighter against her as she nodded. "What do you want to know?"

Kyle spoke into the machine, noting the date, the location, and to whom he was talking. Then, turning his full attention to Meredith, he said, "You can start by telling me who the father of your child is. Then you can tell me why you're so reluctant to make him live up to his legal and moral obligations to you and his child."

4

MEREDITH OBVIOUSLY didn't want to talk about the father of her child. She was clutching her daughter to her bosom as though she half expected someone to snatch the baby away at any moment—as though simply by mentioning the father she were putting the baby in jeopardy.

Kyle betrayed no impatience as he waited for her to speak. Waiting for difficult answers was as much a part of his job as searching for legal precedents or delivering eloquent arguments in court. When that information had to be painfully drawn from his client, the gathering of it became an arduous process.

That's why he kept a box of tissues in his desk drawer.

Eventually, Meredith responded, "Thomas Castor. His name is Thomas Eugene Castor." She separated the words for emphasis.

"*C* or *K*?" Kyle asked.

"*C*." Meredith said. "*C-a-s-t-o-r*, like the oil."

Kyle refrained from commenting on the peculiar comparison. "Address?"

She replied instantly and in complete detail, down to the zip code.

"Do you usually memorize addresses?"

"Not usually. I—" She swallowed, as though the information choked her. "I used to write him letters."

Kyle deliberately sounded noncommittal. "Did he write you letters?"

"Not many," Meredith said. Embarrassed by the admission, she turned her face away from Kyle, then added, defensively, "Thomas wasn't much of a writer."

"Where were you writing to him from?"

"Bloomington, Indiana."

"Is that where you met him?"

"Yes. We were both going to Indiana U. He was working on his masters degree in accounting."

"And you were majoring in home economics."

"Nutrition science," she corrected.

"Tell me about your relationship. How did you meet?"

"I worked at a restaurant near the campus. It was a popular night spot. Lots of students went there—the ones who could afford it."

"What did you do there?"

She laughed softly, as though it amused her that he had to ask. "I waited tables." She hesitated, her laughter gone. "Thomas always sat at one of my tables. It was obvious after a while that he was . . . you know, interested in me."

"And you were interested in him?"

"Yes. I . . ." He'd been nice looking, easygoing. "He was very charming, always talking and joking."

"You dated?"

"Yes."

"You became intimate?"

Meredith scowled at him over Stacy's head. "That's obvious, isn't it?"

"Was it an exclusive relationship?"

"What do you mean?"

"Were either of you seeing other people while you were . . . *involved* with each other?"

"No!" she snapped, insulted. Then, after an awkward pause, she added, "At least, I wasn't, and I don't believe he— I would never have become *involved* with him otherwise."

"Did you ever live together?"

"For a while. Thomas moved into my apartment after he finished his degree. His roommate had graduated, too, and he went home to Indianapolis. Thomas didn't want to pay full rent on a two-bedroom apartment."

"How long did you live at the same address?"

"Over a month. From early January until late February."

"You were intimate during the entire period you lived together?"

"Yes," Meredith said, forcing the word through clenched teeth. She flushed, feeling humiliated by having to detail her private life to this near stranger.

Aware of her discomfort, Kyle said softly, "I have to ask these questions in order to know if we have grounds for a suit. Everything you tell me is privileged information."

"Until we wind up in court."

Kyle didn't reply to that. She was more astute than he'd anticipated. Impatient to get on with the job at hand, he asked, "Were there any understandings between you when you lived together?"

"Understandings?"

"Did you agree that your relationship would be exclusive? Did you anticipate a long-term relationship?"

"I was in love with him," she replied. "I thought . . ." The sentence faded into a forlorn sigh. "Talk about naive."

"What were your expectations?" Kyle pressed. *As if he had to ask. A house in the suburbs, a minivan, PTO meetings and a sheepdog, no doubt.* It was difficult for him to remember that there was a time in his own ancient past when he'd anticipated the same things.

The baby made a gurgling sound. Kyle turned to look at her in time to see Meredith tweak her daughter's tiny nose and smile down at her face. He also recognized the instant when she shifted her attention from the baby back to their discussion; saw the stiffening of her shoulders as she braced herself against the pain of the memories he was forcing her to relive. By the time she raised her head to face him, her demeanor was shockingly different from what it had been just seconds before.

She spoke haltingly, "I thought we'd . . . that he'd get a job, and I'd finish my degree and eventually, we'd—"

"Did you discuss these expectations with Mr. Castor?"

"Not . . . We didn't just sit down and talk about the future, but sometimes it just . . . *came up.* We'd say things like, 'One day we'll do this or that,' or 'Someday we'll have something or other.'"

"Think about this before you answer. Did you both make statements like that, or did you make them and Castor shrug them off?"

Meredith considered the question for a moment. "I never thought about keeping score. Thomas seemed to want . . . expect . . . the same things I expected."

"Can you think of any specific plans you made together?"

After a thoughtful pause, Meredith replied, "We used to talk about how different things would be after he found a job. He'd kiss his résumés for luck before I mailed them and say things like 'This one'll get us a new car,' or 'Here's our ticket to a big-screen TV.'"

Kyle grimaced. She hadn't given him anything yet on which to build a convincing case. New cars and big-screen televisions were bachelor's toys, hardly indicative of nesting. The fact that Castor expected to acquire them when he got a job wouldn't convince even an addle-brained jury that he had been promising to settle down in the suburbs. Kyle tried a more promising angle. "You mailed the résumés for Castor?"

"Usually," Meredith said. "The post office was near the restaurant."

"Did you help him prepare the résumés in any way?"

"Thomas's handwriting was atrocious, so I typed the address labels for him."

A glimmer of hope! By becoming actively involved in his job search, Meredith had contributed to his gaining employment. "Did you type the résumé, too?" Kyle asked.

"Only a rough draft. He had it typeset at a local print shop. I helped him write it, though."

"Before he took it to the print shop."

She nodded. "He gave me the dates and the names and addresses of his employers, and then he'd tell me what his job was and I'd summarize it so that it sounded . . . impressive."

"Did he pay you?"

"Of course not."

"Why do you say it like that? People make good money writing résumés."

"I did it because—" she frowned in frustration "—it was a favor. It never occurred to me to charge him."

"How many résumés did you address for him?"

She shrugged. "Sixty, maybe. He had friends sending him the want ads from several cities. We sent out about a dozen a week."

"Did you ever represent yourselves as husband and wife?"

The question apparently surprised Meredith, and she regarded him with a narrowed gaze for several seconds. Her smoky gray eyes were large, and the dark circles of fatigue under them made them seem even larger. Kyle found her gray stare slightly unnerving. He was relieved when the baby fretted and she turned her attention to soothing her.

"No," she replied.

Kyle had completely lost the train of thought. "No?"

"We never *represented* ourselves as husband and wife."

"But you hoped to marry him."

She made a bitter sound of disgust. "I was in love."

"Did he say that he loved you or imply that he was in love with you?"

"He said . . . affectionate things."

"Be specific."

"He used to tell me—" She faltered, regrouped her thoughts and continued, "He said the things men say to women. That I was special. He called me—" She swallowed as though the words were choking her. "He called me his woman."

"Were you compatible? Did you get along well?"

"Usually. Every once in a while we'd get on each other's nerves. It was never serious, until—"

"Until?" Kyle prompted.

"Until he got a job in Florida and expected me to move with him."

"You didn't want to move?"

"I wanted to wait until after finals, so I didn't lose the whole semester." She sighed in dismay. "Thomas thought I was being unreasonable, that if I loved him the way I said I did, then I'd move with him."

Her eyes met Kyle's and when she spoke again, it was one person talking to another, pleading for human understanding, instead of a client answering an attorney's questions. "It was only a couple of months. I thought he should get settled in Orlando, and I could move down when the semester was over."

"You argued over it."

"Yes. And he moved to Florida in a huff." Her eyes clouded with tears. "I wasn't being unreasonable. I thought when he cooled off he'd realize that. He'd been under such a strain waiting on calls from employers. I thought once he got settled—"

"What about your pregnancy? How did it fit into the scenario?"

She hesitated, thinking before answering. "I began to suspect I was pregnant right after he left for Florida, but I wasn't sure. I thought it could be . . . you know, because I was so upset over his leaving like that."

"The pregnancy was unplanned?"

"That's an understatement. We were . . . we thought we were being safe, but—" Her face colored in embarrassment. "Finally I bought a home test kit, and then went to the clinic on campus."

"How did Castor react when you told him?"

"I didn't tell him right away."

"Didn't you think he deserved to know?"

"I would have told him if he'd been with me. Or if things had been better between us. But he was a long way away, and we . . . I didn't want it to be a factor. I wanted to wait until we'd gotten our relationship

straightened out. I decided to wait until I moved to
Florida to tell him."

"When did you move?"

Meredith shifted the baby from the crook of her arm
onto her shoulder, then patted the infant's back as she
spoke. There was a liquid quality in her voice that betrayed how near tears she was. "As soon as the semester was over. In June."

"Had he encouraged you to join him then?"

"At first . . . He called me after he got here to give me
his address and telephone number and he still sounded
angry. But later, in April, he called to tell me he got the
birthday present I'd sent him, and he was . . . It was like
we were still together. He was very sweet, and he told
me how much he liked the shirt and tie I'd picked out.
He said . . ."

Meredith's voice faltered, and she sucked in a deep
breath before continuing. "He said the reason he hadn't
written or called was because he'd been so busy with
his new job. He said he was working long hours and had
a lot of deadlines."

She responded with disgust in her voice. "He was
busy, all right."

Another woman, Kyle thought, wondering why he
hadn't anticipated it. As a divorce attorney, he'd heard
enough stories from unhappy women to be able to slide
them into categories—infidelity, abuse, or indiffer-
ence—fairly quickly.

Meredith continued, "I almost told him about the
baby during that phone call. We seemed so close again.
But I thought it would be better to deal with something
like that in person."

"Indeed," Kyle murmured dryly. *How nice of you to
call, darling. By the way, I'm pregnant.* The very

thought of such a conversation was enough to strike terror in a man's heart and tie knots in his guts. "What happened when you arrived in Orlando?"

Meredith closed her eyes and bowed her head. Her shoulders sagged with the weight of the memory. She hugged her baby almost fiercely, and then shuddered with the force of a soul-wrenching sigh. She opened her eyes but did not raise them to look at him as she spoke. "Thomas was shocked to see me. I had expected him to be happy. I'd thought he'd grab me and kiss me and tell me . . ."

Tears stole her voice. They slid down her cheeks and dripped onto her blouse, but she appeared not to notice them. "It was obvious he'd never believed I would really come."

With a grunt of inevitability, Kyle turned off the tape recorder, rose, and went off in search of tissue. He returned and slid the box on the table in front of Meredith.

Meredith plucked out a tissue with an obedient air and wiped her cheeks, mumbling a feeble and indistinct "Thanks," followed by an equally indistinct "Sorry."

Kyle waited in impatient silence. Minutes passed before Meredith shifted Stacy from her shoulder back into her lap, then raised her gaze to Kyle's and nodded.

Kyle turned the recorder back on. "Anytime you're ready."

"It was obvious he *wasn't* glad to see me. I asked him what was wrong, and that's when he told me—"

Fresh tears. Kyle turned off the recorder again. "Would you like a glass of water?"

Meredith nodded. She drained the glass he brought her before setting it on the table with a thunk. "Turn the recorder back on," she said with stony resolve. "I'm *through* crying."

Her voice, as she picked up the story, was flat and expressionless. "He said that my showing up was awkward. He actually used that word. *Awkward*, like his stomach had chosen a bad time to rumble or something. You see, the accounting firm he'd gone to work for was privately owned, and his new boss had a daughter."

She stared down at her daughter's face, and poked the baby's palm with her forefinger, then smiled briefly when the child's fingers closed around it.

Watching her, Kyle was struck by the change in her when she responded to her baby. Her escape was brief, however, and as the memories crowded in on her again, she raised her head—not to look at Kyle, but to stare past him, as though she were able to see a great distance instead of the dozen feet to the wall that blocked her view.

"He went to great pains to assure me that the boss's daughter wasn't nearly as pretty as I am . . . *was*. That she wasn't as smart as I was, either, although she already had her degree and was teaching elementary school. But she was crazy about him, and it was an opportunity he couldn't . . . 'screw up,' I believe was the way he put it. He couldn't 'screw up' an opportunity to be the boss's son-in-law and take the express route up the ladder of success."

She leveled that disconcerting gray gaze directly on his face. "I could have accepted it if he'd met someone beautiful and smart and successful and fallen madly in love! But his boss's Plain Jane daughter! He had the *gall* to tell me it was nothing personal."

Wound up by anger, she fumed, "Nothing personal! I'd sold everything that didn't fit in my car and moved out of state to be with him. I gave up my residency in Indiana knowing I'd have to establish residency in Florida before I could go back to school, and God only knows how many hours I'll lose by transferring. And Thomas couldn't *screw up* the chance to marry the boss's homely daughter."

The bitterness in her voice relieved Kyle. Bitterness was the stock-in-trade of aggressive divorce attorneys, and Kyle was among the most aggressive. He flourished as a result of bitterness; and because it was so similar to regret, he had an intimate understanding of it.

Bitterness, to Kyle Sawyer Brooks, was familiar water.

"Is that when you told him about the baby?" he asked.

"No," Meredith replied, sounding tired. "I was too upset. I didn't tell him until several days later, after I'd found a job and an apartment and was moving out. I could tell he was relieved I was leaving. He'd told his girlfriend a friend from college was visiting, and he'd been a nervous wreck that she'd discover it was a female friend and he'd have to do some fast talking."

She laughed bitterly. "When we were living together in Indiana, he'd always been afraid his parents would find out he was living with a female. I don't know why I didn't realize then what a slippery piece of slime he was."

A slippery piece of slime. Bravo, Meredith. We're on our way to the judge! He just had to work out their case. So far, Castor didn't seem to have given them grounds for breech of promise.

In Kyle's opinion, Meredith's naïveté was far more reprehensible. Castor had the motivating forces of greed and opportunism; the only driving force behind Meredith's absurd and reckless behavior was stupidity. Of course, she called it love, but it was a common mistake. Love and stupidity often proved to be interchangeable terms.

"What was his reaction when you told him about your pregnancy?" he asked.

Meredith let out a spate of bitter laughter. "He didn't take the news well."

Kyle cleared his throat to keep from asking her if she'd been expecting a bouquet of posies and a bent-knee proposal in response to her announcement. Just how naive *could* a woman be?

Meredith was staring at the wall again, avoiding meeting his eyes. "He accused me of lying. He said I was making it up, trying to trick him into resuming our relationship."

She drew in a ragged breath. "When I convinced him I wasn't making it up, he said that if I really was pregnant, that it probably wasn't his, that I was trying to..."

Kyle waited in vain for her to finish the thought, then finally prodded her with, "Trying to what, Meredith?"

"That I was trying to stick him with someone else's kid!" she snapped. She turned her head slowly until her gaze met his. The pain reflected in her eyes made him want to look away, but he forced himself to maintain the eye contact she'd established.

"Stick him with a kid," she repeated. "I had loved him. I had lived with him, but I hadn't known him at all. I wouldn't have believed he could be so—callous. His child—our child—and he didn't even care, except that he was afraid he might get *stuck*."

She turned her attention to her daughter then, cradling her in both arms while she caressed the baby's downy scalp with the side of her thumb. The rhythmic stroking continued even as she closed her eyes and a shudder passed through her body. "Then he started in on getting rid of her."

"He wanted you to have an abortion?"

Her breath came rushing out in a gush that oozed agony. "Yes. He called it 'getting rid of it.' Eloquent man, isn't he?"

Kyle correctly interpreted the question as rhetorical and waited for her to go on.

At length, she continued, "He said he'd pay for it if I did, but that if I didn't, I could forget getting any help from him. Ever."

"Why didn't you?"

Meredith's gaze remained fixed on her baby's face, but her thumb ceased its caressing strokes. "I didn't plan on creating another human being, but— I'd read the brochures at the clinic, but—"

She squared her shoulders and raised her chin defiantly. Her eyes met Kyle's with unwavering challenge. "She didn't ask to be conceived, but she was inside me. She was alive. The idea of deliberately destroying . . . I couldn't."

Lord, how persuasive she would be in the witness stand, if he could keep that defiance alive. "In retrospect, it doesn't appear to have been a particularly wise decision."

Her voice was chillingly intense. "You have the gall to look at this beautiful child and say that?"

An awkward silence followed. At length, Meredith said softly, "In retrospect, it was the wisest decision I've ever made. It might well be the only wise decision I've made in the past year."

Kyle stared at her, momentarily stunned. She had succeeded in doing something he'd never have believed possible: she'd shaken him out of his armor of professionalism. He found himself responding judgmentally instead of analytically; as a man instead of as her attorney. "But you're homeless. If you didn't have a baby, you'd be able to work."

"Women with babies have been working since the beginning of time," she told him. "I can work with *mine*. All I needed was a chance."

"I meant that you'd have been healthy and able to work all along, and you wouldn't have ended up—"

"In the streets? Living in my car? Don't pussyfoot around, Mr. Kyle Sawyer Brooks. You said it once. I was homeless. My daughter was homeless. So now you're going to tell me how irresponsible I was not to have destroyed her."

She paused only long enough to draw in a deep breath. "Too bad they did away with debtors' prisons. You could just toss me and the rest of the people stupid enough to find themselves homeless in and let us slowly waste away from hunger and pestilence! Stacy—!"

Her voice cracked as she cupped the baby's tiny foot in her palm. "An ill-conceived 'problem' like Stacy likely wouldn't last more than a few weeks."

Clichés about a mother's love crowded into Kyle's mind. The mother dashing into a burning house to rescue her child. Mothers covering their babies' bodies with their own to shield them from poisonous gas or smoke. Once he'd inadvertently approached a pair of cygnets at Lake Iola park and the mother swan had charged him, hissing and honking horribly, and flapping her wings. He'd admired her courage—the courage to challenge a being ten times her own size, a powerful being with legs that could kick and arms that could flail. He'd admired the courage of that mother swan, and now he discovered within himself a grudging admiration for the woman sitting in front of him. She was neither strong nor wise, but her courage was undeniable.

The air was filled with tension. "I've upset you," he said. "I'm sorry."

Her laughter—bitter, nearly hysterical—violently rent the silence that trailed his apology. "It's a joke, you know?"

"What is?" Kyle asked.

"Pro Choice. They say they're for choice, for women having the right to choose. But when a woman chooses to have a child instead of destroy one—"

"When you made the choice you made, why didn't you sue for support?"

Meredith's jaw dropped. "Where was I supposed to get money for a lawyer? I was barely keeping my head above water as it was, trying to buy vitamins and get ready for a baby."

"But you could have sued for support and medical expenses."

"How was I supposed to prove it was Thomas's child without his cooperation?"

"Surely you had mutual acquaintances, friends who would have sworn that you were living together during the period when the child was conceived."

"I was supposed to drag them down to Florida? Or move back to Indiana and try to do something there? Somehow I can't visualize the state of Indiana dispatching someone to Florida to drag back a man who's run out on the woman he's knocked up."

That disconcerting gray gaze met his again. She had an inner well of strength—or was it dignity?—that mystified him.

"I've been in enough no-win situations to recognize one, Mr. Brooks," she declared.

"There are few legitimate no-win situations, Meredith," he informed her. "And call me Kyle, please. If we're going to be living together..."

He said a curse word, rolled his eyes and pounded buttons on the recorder to stop the tape and rewind it. "I didn't mean that the way— You don't have to worry that— Oh, hell, you know what I meant. I'm Mr. Brooks at the office and in the courtroom, but I'm not going to stand for it in my own house."

He was almost, but not quite, sure he saw Meredith's mouth twitch with a suppressed smile before she said, "You're the boss, *Kyle*."

It bothered Kyle that he wasn't sure about the smile, or about what she found amusing if, in fact she found something amusing. Was it his slip about living together?

Maybe she's mocking you. Maybe she thinks a comment like that on tape could be useful in the future. Maybe behind those eerie gray eyes she's plotting how to murder you in your sleep.

He shrugged off the weird and disturbing thoughts and turned his attention to the recorder, listening to the tape until he reached her comment about the no-win situation, then turning it off briefly before hitting the buttons to begin recording again—over the rest of their previous conversation.

"You're erasing it," Meredith observed.

"Just the part where we got off track."

She made a sound that was noncommittal but significant. He wondered if she realized how his inadvertent comment about living together could be misconstrued and misinterpreted if taken out of context? Was she wily enough to be disappointed that he was erasing it?

"What makes a no-win situation legitimate, Kyle?"

He stared at her blankly for several seconds. "I beg your pardon?"

"I asked what makes a no-win situation legitimate."

She hadn't been thinking about the living-together crack at all, he realized. He switched off the recorder and concentrated on her question.

"You implied that the no-win situation I was in wasn't legitimate," she pressed. "What makes a no-win situation legitimate?"

"Well, it's when no desirable or effective options exist."

"If there were desirable and effective options in my particular situation, I seem to have missed them."

"You allowed yourself to be victimized."

"Allowed?" she parroted in consternation.

"You should have asserted your rights. Instead you chose to become a victim."

"Chose?"

"By not getting tough with Castor, you became a voluntary victim. You were an accomplice to your own victimization, much like people who watch someone being beaten to death and do nothing to stop it."

They faced each other across a silence charged with conviction and outrage. His conviction. Her outrage. He sensed the anger she held in check, the retorts she bit back as she chewed on her bottom lip.

The silence grew long. The tension crescendoed, then fizzled into awkwardness. Meredith exhaled a sigh.

Of relief that she had managed not to vent her anger at him? Or defeat? She was unreadable, an enigma to him. Perversely, he waited for her to speak first.

So he could have the last word? She made him an enigma to himself. It unnerved him. *She* unnerved him—her circumstances, the way she'd been thrust into his life.

But Meredith was not as shrewd as he was, nor as accomplished at the game he was playing. She spoke first.

5

"ARE WE FINISHED?" She punctuated the question with an exhalation that underscored her impatience to be done with the tape recorder and the probing questions.

"No," Kyle said.

Meredith fidgeted in the chair and repositioned the baby on her arm, then looked at him expectantly.

Kyle drew in a lungful of air, then released it slowly. He was about to make her as mad as hell, and he knew it. And dreaded it. "Is there any doubt the baby is Castor's?"

She reacted exactly as he'd predicted. Anger turned her eyes a darker, smoky gray, as she narrowed them. "None."

"How about after Castor left for Florida? Say, within a month to six weeks? Were you with any men then?"

Her chest rose and fell as she breathed deeply and raggedly, trying to hold in her rage.

"If you were—even if they aren't the father—believe me, Castor will find out about them and throw them at you in court. I don't like surprises. If there were men, tell me now."

"I wasn't with any other man," she repeated. "Not . . . ever." She dropped her head and stared at her baby's hands. The portion of her face he could see was covered by a deep flush of humiliation.

"You were a virgin when you met him?" he asked, able to hide only a portion of his surprise.

"Yes." She whipped her head up to face him fully. "He was the first and the only, okay?" After a beat, she added, "And probably the last."

Kyle couldn't suppress a smile. "That's a rash statement for a woman your age. How old *are* you, anyway? Twenty? Twenty-one?"

"Twenty-three."

"And you've already sworn off men."

"Thomas Castor could send a nymphomaniac to a convent."

Grinning, Kyle regarded her curiously. Her sense of humor sneaked up on him. "You'll have a change of heart once you've gotten your life back in order." *Women always did, where men were concerned.*

Meredith gave him a harrumph of disagreement and studied her baby's tiny fingers clenched trustingly around her forefinger. "How old are you?"

"Why do you want to know?"

"Why wouldn't you want to tell me?"

"Twenty-nine," he said flatly.

"That's what I thought."

Kyle waited for her to expand on the statement but she didn't. "*What* did you think?" he asked exasperatedly.

"That you're not really old, you just act that way."

Kyle gave her a down-the-nose paternal scowl that quelled further impertinence and demanded, "Tell me how you came to be living in your car."

He was careful not to look at her face as she composed her answer. He didn't want to see the pain there. He was her attorney, but he didn't want to become involved in her plight, only in the legal aspects of her case. Nevertheless, he heard the anguish in her voice as she recalled, "I couldn't pay my rent."

"Would you elaborate a little?"

She took in a fortifying breath. "Toward the end of my pregnancy, my ankles started swelling because I was on my feet so much. I asked my boss if I could work short shifts, just during the peak lunch and dinner hours, but when he heard the doctor had told me to stay off my feet, he wouldn't let me work at all. He was afraid that if something went wrong with the baby, that . . . I think he was afraid I'd sue him."

"Obviously he didn't know you, or he'd have known there was remote danger of that," Kyle said.

"So I missed a rent payment," Meredith continued. "And then I went a week past my due date, and missed another payment when I was in the hospital. When I got home, there was an eviction notice on the door. Even if I'd gone back to work the day I got out of the hospital, I would have needed three rent payments to keep from getting evicted. I went to the landlady and tried to work out a way to pay extra rent once I went back to work. I offered to do custodial work in the building, even windows, but my landlady said she had a mortgage payment to make on the property and she couldn't make it if she had—" she swallowed "—freeloaders. She said if she made an exception in my case, she'd have a whole building full of shirkers."

She rocked the baby back and forth in her arms. If she had not been holding the infant, Kyle was certain she would be hugging herself and rocking in the same desperate motion. "I'm not a shirker," she told him. "I've never been a shirker."

"Did you contact Castor during this period?"

She nodded. "I didn't know what else to do. I didn't have anyone else to go to."

"No family?"

She shook her head. "The only family I have left is a great-uncle wasting away in a state-owned nursing home, and he doesn't recognize anyone."

"Your parents?"

"Both dead." The words were forced through a tight throat.

"So you called Castor?"

"Yes. To ask for a loan to get me and Stacy through until I could go back to work. I thought that even if he didn't care about me, he'd have some feeling for Stacy, but . . ."

She paused to compose herself. "I thought he'd care, whether he wanted to or not. I didn't see how any human being couldn't care just a little."

A sob broke her speech. She swallowed it and went on. "He didn't even ask her name! He didn't even care what her name was! He said he'd told me where he stood and that if I couldn't take care of a brat, I shouldn't have had one. I asked if he'd at least give me what an abortion would have cost, and he said—"

Her face reflected the shock she still felt over Castor's betrayal as she turned to Kyle in an appeal for understanding—or at least a validation that her expectations had been reasonable. "He said that if he helped me once, I'd just be back again and again and he'd never get rid of me. He said I was trying to mess things up with his fiancée. He made me sound like a blackmailer, like a scum-of-the-earth criminal. That's why—"

"Why you didn't want to press him for help?" Kyle demanded in an accusatory tone. "Because he made you feel as though you were inconveniencing him, like you were the one at fault? Maybe you didn't know him, but he sure as hell must have known you. He knew all the right buttons to push."

Half a minute passed in awkward silence before Kyle said, "He was aware that you and his child were in imminent danger of eviction and he refused to help you."

Meredith's only response was a continuation of stony silence.

Kyle was tempted to ask her if she realized that Castor's fear that his fiancée would find out about her and the baby gave her power over him. He wanted to shake her because she hadn't had the guts or gumption to storm into Castor's office and demand help. He asked, "Why didn't you get more aggressive with him?"

"He'd made it clear how he felt about the baby. I made the decision to go through with the pregnancy knowing that. It didn't seem fair—"

"Was it fair for you and the baby to be destitute when the baby's father was sitting fat and happy with money earned from a job you helped him get?"

Meredith's throat convulsed as she swallowed, but she said nothing.

"Are you still in love with him?"

She took a long time to answer. "No," she finally said, and sighed. "I don't love him anymore. How could anyone love a . . . *monster*? I'm just . . . ashamed that I was ever foolish enough to love him, to let him..."

Stoically, Kyle pushed the box of tissue within her reach and then, with a sigh, jabbed the button on the tape recorder. "That's enough for now. You've got excellent grounds for suing for support during your pregnancy, for medical expenses and child support."

"Will we end up in court?"

"We could. But I suspect Castor'll deal with us before it goes that far. Once he knows you're serious and that you have legal counsel, he's going to want to settle this as quickly and quietly as possible."

"His fiancée's going to find out."

"It's your best leverage against him. He'll deal with us to keep that from happening. His greed will make him malleable."

"I didn't want it to be this way. This ugly."

"I don't imagine you wanted to end up in the streets, either," he replied.

After a long silence, he said, "It's his child, too, and he has a legal and moral responsibility to it."

"Her."

Kyle gave Meredith a questioning look.

"Stacy's a her, not an it. She's a human being."

"Castor has a legal and moral responsibility to *her*," Kyle amended. "And you owe it to her to make him live up to those responsibilities even if you're uncomfortable with the idea of making Castor's life a little complicated."

Meredith nodded gravely, but Kyle suspected that if the circumstances had been different, that if she had walked into his office for a preliminary consultation, she'd never have paid him a second visit.

"THERE'S A WOMAN named Meredith on line one who says she's your housekeeper," Mitzi said. "Do you want to take the call?"

Kyle frowned. Meredith was shopping for furniture for the maid's quarters and he'd given her his office number with the suggestion that she call if she had any problems using his credit card. Another hassle. "I'd better take it."

"This is the second time she's called, but you said you didn't want to be disturbed when you were with Mrs. Collier, so I asked her to call back," Mitzi informed him. "Should I have put her through?"

"No. You did just fine."

Reluctantly, Kyle punched the lighted button. After the morning he'd had, it was probably expecting too much to hope that this telephone call was anything that could be handled simply. "Meredith?"

Meredith answered with a hesitant hello, then, "Kyle?"

"What's up?"

"I bought a mattress and springs for the bed," she said. "They'll be delivered later this week."

"That's good."

"I, uh—"

Here comes the bombshell, Kyle thought as he waited for her to continue.

"I didn't find a chest of drawers at the furniture store but when I was buying the paint for the bed, I got to talking to the clerk and she told me about a used-furniture store nearby, and I found a beautiful chest of drawers there. I can paint it to match the bed and it'll be perfect."

"Good," Kyle said, still waiting for the din of an exploding bombshell.

"It was seventy-five dollars, but I talked them down to sixty," Meredith told him.

"Sounds like a bargain."

"Cash."

"Cash?"

"They don't take credit cards, and since I bought groceries yesterday and paint this morning, there's not that much cash left out of what you gave me yesterday." She hesitated, then added anxiously, "I could have them hold it, then find your office and come back for it."

Sighing, Kyle looked at his watch. It wasn't quite noon, and he didn't have to be at the courthouse until three o'clock. "That won't be necessary. Tell me where you are and I'll meet you there."

After hanging up, he counted the cash in his wallet, then took his suit coat from the clothes rack in his office and walked to the reception area. "I'm going out for a while, Mitzi."

Mitzi nodded, then added nonchalantly, "I didn't know you had a housekeeper, Kyle."

"I just hired her."

"She sounds nice."

"Just a bag lady who needed a job," he said dryly, hoping to sidetrack Mitzi's curiosity with humor.

"She sounded awfully young for a bag lady."

"Apparently there's no minimum age," Kyle remarked. Then, slinging his coat over his shoulder, he left before Mitzi could fish for more information.

MEREDITH SAT in a rocking chair in the back corner of Dot's Used Furniture, waiting for Kyle's arrival. Beneath a gauzy veil of a freshly laundered diaper tossed over her shoulder for privacy, she was nursing a ravenous Stacy while the owner of the shop, Dot, a retired schoolteacher, kept an eye on the door.

"I'm glad young mothers are nursing again," Dot said. "For a long time it wasn't fashionable, but anything so natural has to be good for the baby."

"It is," Meredith responded. "It's supposed to give the baby immunity to a lot of diseases."

Dot smiled. "My daughter and daughter-in-law both nursed their children, and they all flourished. My youngest grandchild is nine now."

"Do they live nearby?" Meredith asked.

"No, they're all back in Ohio. We moved down here when John—that's my husband—retired a couple of years ago. He likes the year-round golf."

"You must miss them."

"Yes. But then, they're all busy with school and gymnastics and music lessons. We get to spend quality time with them twice a year. My oldest granddaughter is talking about spending summers with us and working at Disney when she's old enough."

"That should be fun for her," Meredith said. "I plan on applying for full-time work in one of the big hotels as soon as Stacy is old enough for day care."

"Oh? Don't you like the job you have now?"

"It's . . . just temporary," Meredith explained.

"Oh." Dot obviously was slightly puzzled, but she didn't pry for more information. Instead, she applied her energy and attention to scrubbing the vinyl upholstery of a sofa she was readying for display in the store.

A few minutes later she asked, "Does your boss drive a gray sedan?"

Embarrassed to admit she hadn't noticed what color car her employer drove, Meredith searched for a suitable reply, but was spared having to answer when Dot continued, "If so, he just turned into the parking lot."

"Perfect timing," Meredith commented, fumbling with the fastener of her nursing bra under the diaper. "Stacy just went to sleep."

By the time Kyle had reached the shop entrance, Meredith was standing, cradling Stacy on her shoulder. She nodded a greeting. "The chest of drawers is over here," she said. "If you open the drawers you'll see it has tongue-and-groove joints, and dust shelves under each drawer."

"I'm sure it's fine," Kyle answered brusquely. "Who do I pay?"

"I'm always happy to take money," Dot interjected, poising a pen over the machine that dispensed sales slips. "That'll be sixty dollars plus tax."

Kyle drew three twenties and a five from his wallet and laid them on the counter. Dot picked them up. "The little lady's quite a haggler," she commented. "Talked me down from seventy-five."

Kyle shot Meredith an irritated scowl, then turned to Dot. "We can pay full price," he offered, reaching for his wallet again.

Dot laughed. "Put that away. I was complimenting her. Haggling's half the fun in the used-furniture business—for the seller as well as the buyer."

"If you're sure," he replied dubiously.

"Quite sure. Of course, I wouldn't mind sweetening my day's take by selling you that rocker. It has a forty-dollar tag, but I'll throw it in for thirty."

"Rocker?"

"The one she just got out of. She and the baby looked right at home in it. A little spit and polish and a cushion, and it would be pretty, as well as useful."

Kyle considered the suggestion, then turned to Meredith. "Would you like the chair?"

"It would be convenient, but—"

"There's space enough for it in your room, isn't there?"

"I guess . . . Yes. There's room."

"Do you want it? If you'd like to have it to rock the baby, then get it."

Shrugging whimsically, Meredith told Dot, "We'll take it."

Kyle counted out two more twenties. As Dot reached into her cash drawer for change, he turned to Meredith. "I hate to rain on any parades, but it just occurred to me to wonder how you're going to get this stuff to the house."

"The chest will fit in the trunk if I tie down the lid. The chair—" She thought for several seconds. "If the chair doesn't fit upside down on the back seat, I guess it'll have to go on the roof."

An expression of strong disapproval crept over Kyle's face.

"It's not far to the house," Meredith continued. "We can tie it down securely."

"You can't go through the neighborhood looking like you've driven out of an episode of *The Beverly Hillbillies*."

Meredith's cheeks reddened. "Let's see if it'll fit in the back seat. If not, we just won't get it."

"I've got a suggestion," Dot interjected. "The young man who works at the convenience store next door has a truck. He makes deliveries for fifteen dollars per trip."

"Done!" Kyle said, expecting Meredith to be pleased. But she looked more forlorn than delighted. He gave Dot detailed directions to his house and his home phone number so she could call them and let them know when the furniture would be delivered, then followed Meredith out of the shop and to her car.

"Aren't you happy about the furniture?" he asked.

"Yes, but—"

"I thought it was what you wanted for your quarters."

After several seconds of silence, she said, "I don't mean to keep embarrassing you."

"Embarrassing me?"

"By haggling over prices, or going through your neighborhood looking like a hillbilly."

Damn! He'd hurt her feelings. "I didn't mean that the way it sounded," he told her. "I was more concerned about safety than anything else. What if you'd tied it to the top of the car and it had slipped off?"

"I would have tied it securely," Meredith insisted. "I may be poor, but I'm not a dithering idiot."

"It's a moot point now," he said tersely, then added, "you wouldn't want to dent up the top of your car, anyway."

Meredith gave her car a significant once-over from front to rear fenders, then gave Kyle a look that made him feel ridiculous. The car wasn't exactly a wreck, but it was hardly a used-car salesman's dream trade-in, either. She walked to the door on the passenger side and opened it, then gently lowered Stacy into the infant seat, trying not to wake her as she fastened the straps.

"She's really zonked, huh?" Kyle commented awkwardly.

"I fed her while I was waiting on you. She usually sleeps a couple of hours this time of day."

With Stacy secured, Meredith gently closed the car door and started toward the driver's side.

"One of my favorite restaurants is just around the corner," Kyle said. "I don't eat Tex-Mex very often, but sometimes I'm just in the mood for it. Why don't you follow me and we'll grab some lunch."

"I don't . . . I'm not . . ." Meredith looked from her T-shirt and jeans to Kyle's suit pants, starched shirt, and tie.

"It's casual," Kyle told her. "Tex-Mex."

"I was planning on making a sandwich at the house," she replied, still hedging.

"Come on. You've saved me hundreds of dollars today. The least I can do is spring for lunch."

He smiled and the transformation was amazing. He seemed younger, less staid; his face looked almost boyish. Meredith glimpsed something new in him: charm.

"Lead on, then," she said, and, while starting her car, murmured under her breath, "I never pass up a free meal."

As he'd promised, the restaurant was casual, the lunch clientele an eclectic crowd of professionals, blue-collar workers and housewives taking a break from shopping. A harried waitress thunked a bowl of piquante sauce and a basket of tortilla chips on their table and took their drink orders, then pointed out the menus propped between the salt-and-pepper shakers.

Kyle dipped a chip into the red sauce. "Have you ever eaten Tex-Mex?"

"Once or twice."

"I hope you like spicy food." He ate the sauce-soaked chip.

"I do," Meredith said. "I just hope Stacy does, too."

Kyle looked at the baby sleeping in the infant seat. "She's too little for regular food, isn't she?"

Realizing he was completely serious, Meredith chuckled. "I wasn't going to stuff a tortilla in her mouth! She gets anything I eat, indirectly. I haven't eaten anything spicy since I've been nursing, but some babies get colicky when their mothers eat onions or garlic or any kind of pepper. I'd better take it easy on the piquante." To illustrate, she dipped only the corner of one of the triangular chips into the sauce before nibbling at it.

They ordered combination plates. In the pall of silence that fell over the table in the wake of the waitress's departure, Kyle studied the woman who'd been thrust into his life. Her light brown hair was slicked back into a ponytail at her nape. It was a style often worn by fashion models, and he supposed some women would envy her her good cheekbones—except that the hollows in her cheeks were too pronounced, and the dark circles under her eyes made her look tired and defeated instead of chic. He wondered what thoughts were shaping her generous mouth into such a grim line.

"You've had a busy morning," he commented.

Meredith snapped to attention and nodded. "And I'm going to have a busy afternoon if Stacy will cooperate. I'd like to get the bed sanded down and ready to paint first thing in the morning. Then I can put on the second coat tomorrow afternoon and have the bed together by the time the mattress and spring arrive."

"You're very industrious."

"Force of habit, I guess." She paused, absently chewing on her bottom lip, then said, seriously, "I'm sorry I disturbed you at the office. I could have come back and paid Dot tomorrow."

Kyle shrugged. "You caught me on a good day." He forced a smile. "Besides, this way, you ended up with the rocker and I got Tex-Mex for lunch."

The smile again. Another dose of the boyish charm. She could almost like Kyle Sawyer Brooks when he wasn't playing lawyer. "If you like chili, I'll make it sometime," she offered.

"That would be nice."

"For an Indiana Yankee, I make great chili. I use cubed meat instead of hamburger and let it simmer all day. Do you like your chili with beans, or without?"

Kyle took the question as rhetorical and didn't reply; unnerved by his lack of response, Meredith chattered on. "It's not a question people compromise on. Most people like it either with, or without, and they don't like it the other way at all."

Her attempt at cheerfulness wore on Kyle's nerves. "You don't have to be so . . . overzealous, Meredith."

"I just want to do a good job," she answered softly.

"You're trying too hard."

Frustrated, she said irritably, "Sorry."

Kyle's exasperation equaled Meredith's frustration. "I'm not going to fire you and bounce you back out into the street, you know."

They sat in tense silence until a sheepish smile played at Kyle's mouth. "I can take or leave the beans. Just don't ever try to feed me anything with mushrooms in it."

Surprise registered on Meredith's face. "You don't like mushrooms?"

"Mushrooms are a fungus, like athlete's foot."

Meredith grimaced. "Beef Stroganoff will never be the same."

"Beef Stroganoff can be anything it wants to be," Kyle responded, then added pointedly, with a down-the-nose glare for emphasis, "as long as it doesn't turn up on my table."

"That seems simple enough," Meredith said.

"I'm a simple man."

Meredith considered the remark a moment, then looked him straight in the eye. "I don't think you're a simple man. I think you're a very complicated man."

Kyle raised an eyebrow but refrained from comment when the waitress brought their lunch, and he and Meredith turned their attention to their food.

After facing the challenge of a taco with a crumbling shell, avalanching cheese and lettuce and meat with dripping sauce, Meredith progressed to the more manageable meat-and-cheese enchiladas. It was such a treat being in a restaurant as a customer, eating well-prepared, tasty food. She wanted to tell Kyle as much, and was contemplating the most appropriate way, when he asked, "What makes you think I'm complicated?"

Meredith considered the question, so deceptively simple on the surface, yet so difficult to answer. "There are so many mysteries about you," she replied.

"Mysteries?"

"Discrepancies."

Kyle placed his fork on his plate and sat back in his chair at attention, waiting for an explanation. Meredith put down her own fork. "You're rather...well, formidable."

His eyebrow rose again.

"I can't figure out why you hired me. You didn't want to. That was obvious. I mean, it wasn't exactly a spontaneous gesture of generosity. You were about as cheerful as a man in leg irons when we left the rectory. I thought it was because Father Mark asked you to give me a job, and you did it because...well, because he was your priest. But the man who brought the truck said he knew almost every member of Father Mark's congregation, and he'd never heard of you, so if you're a member of the flock, you're the sheep who's been lost in the wilderness."

Kyle's mouth tensed, and his expression darkened with anger. Meredith drew in a fortifying breath before going on.

"You're not the type to be easily intimidated, yet for some reason, you let Father Mark strongly *influence* you."

"Manipulate me, you mean."

"I don't know," Meredith confessed. "It's just . . . exactly what I said—a mystery."

"A mystery that's not up for discussion," he said tersely. "And what other little discrepancies have you discovered about me?" As if to demonstrate that he wasn't taking the conversation too seriously, he picked up his fork, popped a generous mouthful of enchilada into his mouth, and chewed with feigned nonchalance while waiting for her response.

"You don't like me much, but you're helping me file a suit against Thomas," she replied.

Something that might qualify as concern flashed across his face. "What makes you think I don't like you?"

Meredith sniffed exasperatedly. "*Like* was the wrong word. I should have said *respect*." She gave a bitter, self-deprecating half laugh. "I guess from your point of view there's not a lot about me to respect."

Kyle looked extremely uncomfortable. She wasn't sure why—possibly because, whether his help came reluctantly or not, she was deeply indebted to him— Meredith felt a compelling need to alleviate the discomfort she'd put him in. But the urge passed when he spoke up defensively.

"Respect is earned. If you don't respect yourself enough to demand your rights, if you let yourself be victimized, I don't see how you can expect anyone else to respect you."

So much for benevolence, Meredith thought, trying not to show the anguish his censure caused her. His gaze caught hers, inviting her to defend herself— *Begging* her to defend herself.

"Everything's easy when you're looking at it from the outside, from a detached, legal point of view," she said softly. "It's not so easy when you're involved, when you're living a situation."

He silently resumed eating.

Meredith resumed eating, too, but only because she appreciated having food in front of her and remembered too well what it was like not to have it. Her pleasure in being at the restaurant had evaporated, thanks to Kyle's disapproval.

They exchanged curt mutual goodbyes in the parking lot. Meredith ached with disappointment as she drove back to Kyle's house. Even her excitement over the bargains she'd found had dissipated after the unsettling discussion with Kyle. He'd been so charming when he'd invited her to lunch, and she'd been enjoying herself before the conversation had turned sour.

While sanding the head- and footboards of the old bed, she tried to figure out why his opinion of her rankled so much. She wasn't trying to impress anyone—especially a pompous attorney. She was just trying to survive. So long as she had a job and a roof over her head and Stacy's, what did it matter what Mr. No-Mushrooms-on-My-Table thought of her?

It just matters.

Whether it was pride, self-esteem or dignity that made her care about his opinion, she wasn't sure. Whatever the reason, it did seem to matter to her what the man with the resources to keep her off the streets until she was truly self-sufficient thought of her. If he respected her, then everything he'd done for her could be construed as help. Without his respect, it became charity—not the charity equated with love for one's fellow man, but the kind of patronizing charity that demeaned its recipient.

She rubbed the fine sandpaper over the wooden headboard with savage thrusts as she mulled over the enigma of Mr. Kyle No-Mushrooms Brooks. He was good-looking, polite, intelligent and confident; *and* arrogant, insensitive and inflexible.

A simple man? What a joke! He wore an armor of haughty detachment and superciliousness. And yet— he'd given her a job. He was helping her.

Why?

Meredith was no closer than before to an answer to the riddle when Stacy awoke from her nap hungry and anxiously let the world know about it. Meredith dropped her sandpaper and brushed the powdered paint off her T-shirt, then dashed inside to comfort and feed her wailing daughter.

6

Kyle sat in his car for several minutes after shutting off the engine, delaying the inevitable. The last thing he wanted to do after the way lunch had ended today was walk inside his house and face the near stranger who'd been thrust into his life. He dreaded entering his own home—another thing to thank Mark for the next time he saw him.

Reluctantly Kyle opened the car door and got out. An orange cat approached him, meowing. Just what he needed! The stray had been trying to take up residence at the house for a couple of weeks. He stomped his foot and waved his hands menacingly. "Scat! Go on. Get out of here."

Kyle watched the cat scurry away. If that cat kept hanging around, he was going to have to call Animal Control to haul her off.

The kitchen was empty, but he could hear a baby's angry cries from somewhere in the interior of the house. Was it just days ago when he hadn't dreaded going into his own home, when he didn't have to feel defensive about his commonsense attitude toward life, when his house had been a calm, quiet place to be?

The racket was coming from the guest room. Kyle trotted past the open door, hoping to avoid an encounter with Meredith, and cloistered himself in the privacy of the master bedroom, where he showered and dressed for the casual dinner he'd planned with two fellow attorneys he'd run into at the courthouse.

He was not looking forward to the evening of legal banter, Buffalo wings and flirting waitresses in short skirts, but he was grateful for the convenient excuse not to stay at home and be subjected to Meredith's nervous chatter over dinner.

The baby was still crying as Kyle slapped on his after-shave. If he were lucky, he decided, Meredith would be busy enough quieting the infant that he could make it through the house without running into her. He'd leave her a note on the kitchen table telling her he'd be eating with friends and wouldn't be home until late.

His luck ran out just as he reached the end of the hallway. The baby's cries seemed louder just before Meredith's voice stopped him in his tracks.

"I thought I heard you," she said.

Caught, he turned and nodded an obligatory greeting.

"Dinner's not ready yet," she told him, "but I put some chicken breasts in to marinate this morning, so it shouldn't take long...."

"I'm going out," he announced. "It looks as though you have your hands full, anyway. Is she okay?"

Meredith glanced down at her screaming daughter. "She's never been this fussy before. It's probably just a touch of colic. I gave her a bath, thinking that might soothe her, but obviously it didn't do the trick."

"I won't be back until late," Kyle added, then took advantage of Meredith's preoccupation with Stacy as the child let out a particularly shrill cry to slip away.

Kyle was surprised to hear the baby crying when he returned to the house just before midnight. He tiptoed through the hallway, noting the bar of light coming from under the closed door as he passed the guest room. His conscience—and an unexpected stab of concern—made him stop, turn back and knock softly on the door.

It opened almost immediately. Meredith was holding Stacy on her shoulder. She appeared frazzled as she patted the screaming infant on the back. "You're home," she said.

"I couldn't help hearing," Kyle explained, suddenly feeling self-conscious.

"I'm sorry. I've tried everything to get her to stop crying."

Kyle frowned. "Has she been screaming like that the whole time I was gone?"

Desperation turned Meredith's eyes a deeper shade of gray as she nodded. "I'll take her into the maid's quarters so she won't keep you awake," she offered.

He dismissed the suggestion with a shake of his head. "I'm not worried about sleeping. Is she all right?"

"I think it's just colic. It must be the spicy food I ate. She slept until late afternoon. Then, about half an hour after I fed her, she started screaming."

"Do you want to take her to a doctor? There's a twenty-four-hour clinic not far from here."

"She doesn't have any fever, and she's not dehydrated."

"Don't worry about the expense," Kyle said. "If you think she needs to go, I'll take care of it."

"If I'd thought she was in any real danger I'd have taken her in myself by now. I really think it's just colic. Babies just fuss sometimes. The spicy food probably gave her a tummyache, and then she got wound up and swallowed a lot of air, and that made the problem worse. She's probably as frustrated as I am by this point."

"If you're sure," Kyle replied, wondering if he should insist on taking the baby to the clinic. Meredith seemed confident and competent with the child, but she didn't look any too well herself. Her gray eyes were ashen and appeared deeper-set than usual.

"Is there anything I can do?" he asked, feeling utterly useless in the face of the bawling babe and exhausted mother.

"Thanks, but—" Meredith hesitated. She chewed on her bottom lip, obviously reconsidering her hasty refusal of his offer to help.

"What can I do?" he asked.

"If you really don't mind, maybe you could hold her a few minutes while I mix up some of the formula Father Mark gave us. It's the only thing I haven't tried, and she could be hungry by now, after the workout she's had."

"I don't mind, but—" Kyle was humiliated by the blush he felt spreading hotly over his face. "I've never held a baby before," he confessed. "You'll have to show me how."

"It's easy," Meredith replied. "But are you sure you want to do this?"

"If you think it'll help."

"It will. If you think she's screaming now, you should hear her when I put her down. I'll get a fresh diaper for your shoulder."

Kyle watched her balancing act with interest as she anchored the bawling baby on her shoulder with one hand and dug through the bag of baby things she carried around with the other. As she slapped the folded cloth diaper over his shoulder he grinned and asked, "I don't know much about babies, but don't diapers go a little lower?"

She smoothed and straightened the diaper with her palm and fingertips. Despite the efficiency of her movements, he noticed that her touch was gentle—a mother's touch.

"The way she's been crying, she could spit up," Meredith explained. "I wouldn't want her to get your shirt dirty."

"Oh," Kyle said. He'd had a friend once who, in the days of his early fatherhood, had told him that babies always had something disgusting coming out one end or the other. His enthusiasm for actually *touching* the baby was waning, but he could see no way out.

"You really don't know how to hold a baby?" Meredith questioned.

He shook his head.

"Spread out your arms," she instructed. "Not that far, just a few inches away from your body. Good. Now, we'll figure out the best way—" She lowered Stacy into her arms, cradling her head in the crook of her elbow. Then, raising her arm, she placed Stacy's face against Kyle's chest, then eased her upward until the baby's head rested high on his shoulder.

She had to raise her arms level with her own ears to hold the baby there. "I never realized you were so tall."

"What do I do?" Kyle asked, fighting panic as he felt the warmth and movement of the baby, and the screams assaulted his ear with almost deafening volume.

Meredith guided his left hand to the baby's bottom. Spreading her hand over his, she showed him how to anchor the baby to him by cupping the roundness there. "Your hands are so big!" she said. "This should be easy for you."

Kyle made a doubting sound.

"Now, with this one—" She raised his right hand and pressed it gently over the baby's back, urging it into a position where he supported Stacy's neck. "Good," she told him and, sensing his panic, smiled. "See? It *is* simple with such big hands. You can pat her back or rub it. The important thing is not to let her arch backward or let her head wobble."

"Don't let the head wobble," Kyle repeated, committing the instruction to memory. "Is she always this loud?"

"Only when she's upset," Meredith said, with the hint of a smile. Obviously she found his inexperience amusing. Kyle wasn't sure he found her amusement at his expense amusing.

"Come on to the kitchen. I'll mix up the formula."

"I can walk around with her? It's safe?"

"As long as you don't let her head wobble or her back arch. She'll probably enjoy the ride. Just . . . try to relax a little, or she'll pick up on your tension."

Relax? With a siren going off in his ear and the awesome responsibility of keeping a wiggling mass of flesh and bone from wobbling or bending the wrong way? She had to be kidding. He took a tentative step to follow her, then sighed with relief to discover that his legs worked as usual despite the weight and responsibility balanced on his shoulder, literally and figuratively.

A funny thing happened on the way down the hallway: Stacy's cries grew less strident, less continuous. *That's better,* Kyle thought, relieved by the intermittent spells of quiet sandwiched between piercing screams. As Kyle crossed the high-ceilinged living room, Stacy rooted her head against his shoulder and her screams turned into odd, irregular snuffles.

"Is this normal?" he asked Meredith, upon entering the kitchen. Instinctively he whispered, afraid that the sound of his voice might startle the child. "She sounds different."

Meredith stared at him wide-eyed. "I don't believe it," she whispered back. Then, demonstrating with her hand, she said, "Pat her back." She grimaced. "Easy. Gently. Yeah, like that."

The baby snuffled again and made a sound like a deflating balloon. "What's happening?" Kyle asked.

"She's not crying anymore," Meredith reported. "Just keep moving."

The snuffling gradually eased into the rhythm of normal breathing interrupted by an occasional hiccup. Meredith had finished mixing the formula and prepared a bottle, but she left it on the counter and devoted her full attention to Stacy and Kyle. "Whatever you do, don't make any sudden movements or loud noises."

"Is something wrong?"

Meredith shook her head. "Her eyes are closed. She's going to sleep."

"She's not passing out or anything?" Kyle asked warily.

Meredith laughed softly. "No. She's just drifting off."

A few minutes later, Meredith announced, "She's zonked. The crying must have worn her out."

"I don't understand," Kyle replied. "You'd been holding her for hours."

"She feels secure with you," Meredith explained.

"But how . . . why?"

"You're warm and strong. She sensed your strength."

"What do I do now?"

"If you don't mind holding her, it might be better if you just held her a little while longer, let her get a little more deeply asleep before you try to put her down."

"Okay."

"You could sit down," Meredith suggested. "I'll get us something to drink. Milk?"

"Water will do for me."

"Actually, I feel like a sandwich," Meredith said. "I'm famished after fighting with her all night."

"You didn't get any dinner?"

Meredith gave him a you've-got-to-be-kidding look. "I'm not even sure I was breathing half the time." She set a glass of ice water in front of him, then went to the pantry for tuna and proceeded to make tuna salad. "Can I fix one for you?" she asked, as she opened the bread wrapper.

"No, thanks. I had about a ton and a half of Buffalo wings at the restaurant."

"I could eat a whole buffalo right now," Meredith commented.

Kyle watched her center the sandwich she'd just made on a plate and cut it into two perfect triangles. She worked with practiced, economical movements.

"You're very much at home in a kitchen," he observed.

"I ought to be," she told him. "I've been cooking for as long as I can remember, and I've worked at enough delis and restaurants to know how to run my own."

"Is that why you were majoring in—what did you call it?"

"Nutrition science." Meredith put the milk carton from which she was pouring on the counter and shrugged. "There was no restaurant-management program in the area, so nutrition was the best compromise. You get restaurant jobs on experience anyway, so I'll have that to combine with my degree."

"You want to work in a restaurant?"

"Uh-hmm. Or for a caterer. Actually, I'd like to start a catering service, but that's a few years down the road."

Stacy snuffled and burrowed against Kyle's shoulder in her sleep. He instinctively stroked her back. She was very warm and surprisingly heavy lying there on his shoulder. He looked down at her and his chin rubbed against the soft, fine down that covered her scalp, and he wondered if the sweet scent of that hair was attributable to special baby soap.

He marveled that a human being could be so tiny and so trusting. She'd accepted the strength and human warmth of a total stranger as comfort. The innocence inherent in that acceptance moved him beyond words. He had not realized such innocence existed in the world; she had fallen asleep while cradled in his hands—and had touched his heart in the process.

Meredith sat down with her sandwich and glass of milk. Kyle watched her attack the sandwich with gusto and wash the first half down with milk. "Did you come from a large family?" he asked.

She shook her head. "No. Why?"

"You seem to know a lot about babies."

"I did a lot of baby-sitting when I was a teenager." She picked up the second half of her sandwich.

He remembered when he had blithely discussed having children. So long ago. A lifetime ago. Years ago—years that might have been millennium. He and Shannon had been like characters in a romance, talking about children as part of the happily-ever-after ending. They were going to have children who would look like them and adore them. Had they ever thought about having babies that cried for hours on end? "You must have known what you were getting into," he said, thinking aloud.

Meredith turned that knowing gray gaze on him, the one that gave him the uncomfortable suspicion that she could see into his mind. "Did you think I thought I was getting some living baby doll who'd be mine and adore me? That's what fourteen-year-olds think when they get pregnant. I wasn't fourteen." She sighed. "I'm not sure I was ever fourteen—not *that* kind of fourteen."

Kyle couldn't think of any suitable response. Then Stacy made a smacking sound similar to a kiss as she moved her lips in a suckling motion in her sleep. Meredith looked at her daughter's face and smiled; Kyle was again awed by the sweetness of the baby.

"You think I was grossly irresponsible to have had her," Meredith stated. "But I wasn't. I've been working full-time since I was eighteen, and I worked after school and weekends before that. I knew I could take care of a baby, and I honestly believed at the time that I could provide for her. I wasn't a high-school dropout. I had three years of college, and I'd been working all my life. I never thought—"

Sliding her plate aside, she propped her elbow on the table, her chin on her palm, and sighed. "No one really thinks it'll happen to them. *Homeless.* My God. I would never even have imagined it. I couldn't even *believe* it when it was happening. It was incomprehensible. It wouldn't have happened if I hadn't had to quit working. I'd have worked if my boss had let me, even full-time. But once I'd told him what the doctor had said—"

"Don't you have family or friends? Someone—any-one—who would have helped you?"

"I don't have any family left," she answered, her eyes haunted by a sadness that made Kyle uncomfortable. "And I have a friend here, another waitress at the restaurant. I stayed with her for a few days after I was evicted, but the man she lived with . . ."

A faraway look crept into her eyes, but the sadness remained. "Two was company, and three was a crowd, if you get my drift. And when the third party had a baby that cried . . ."

She closed her eyes, trying to shut out unpleasant memories, but couldn't.

"He didn't like the baby crying at night. Once, when he was hung over and Stacy woke him up, he started cursing at my friend. She told him that I didn't have anywhere else to go, and he . . . he *hit* her. The next day when she was at work, I apologized to him. I said I would leave as soon as I found a place to go and he . . ."

She swallowed. "He looked at me in a way that made me feel cheap and dirty, and told me that *maybe* I didn't have to be in such a hurry, that *maybe* I could change his attitude if I was 'nice' to him. That's when I left."

"He sounds almost as charming as Castor."

"He just didn't bother with the sheep's clothing," Meredith explained. She stood and carried the dishes to the sink, rinsed them and put them in the dishwasher before turning back to Kyle. "She shouldn't wake up if you lay her down now."

Kyle followed her to the guest room and waited while she pulled back the covers of the portable bassinet. "I'm not sure how to move her," he said.

"Brace her with both hands, one on her bottom and the other spread over her back and neck," Meredith instructed. "Now, bend over from the waist, so her weight will settle into your hands."

Stacy jerked in her sleep, flinging her arms wide, and Kyle jumped. "Careful," Meredith whispered. "Lay her down and gently roll her over onto her tummy."

"I have to roll her over?"

"Babies are less likely to choke on their tummies."

Kyle nodded and eased Stacy onto her stomach, then smiled triumphantly as she snuggled into the mattress without waking.

"Thank you for holding her," Meredith said.

Kyle smiled sheepishly. "It was an experience. I'm glad I could help."

He turned to leave. "The diaper!" Meredith exclaimed, reaching up to take it away. Kyle reached for it, too, and his hand brushed over hers. Her slender fingers were warm and nimble. He was aware of her suddenly not as an annoyance who'd been thrust into his life, not as a hapless victim—but as a woman.

Wrong! You don't need trouble, and she's trouble with a capital T. Still, he felt reluctant to take his hand away. When he finally did, he studied her face, wondering about the mysteries hidden in the gray depths of her eyes.

7

MEREDITH WAS PUTTING the first coat of paint on the headboard of the bed when the cat ambled up to the screened-in patio and meowed. It was a tabby, orange with white stripes tinged with the merest hint of gray. Satisfied that he had Meredith's attention, he sat down, wrapped his tail around his hind legs and meowed again.

"Hello, yourself," Meredith replied, grinning at the cat's stance. "Where'd you come from? You live around here?"

The cat gave her an eerie, unblinking stare.

"Giving me the aloof treatment, eh?" Meredith said. "Very well, don't talk to me." She dipped the paintbrush into the paint and then stroked it over the headboard with even, overlapping strokes, glancing at the cat sideways as she worked.

The cat got up, walked to the screen and brushed up against it several times. Meredith chuckled. *Works every time!* She'd never seen a cat yet that could stand to be ignored.

The cat sat down again, close to the screen.

"What's your name?" Meredith asked, as though the cat might answer. "You look like a rogue to me. You'd need a rough name. Shall I call you Bruno? Mack? I know—Champ."

The cat meowed. "You like that one, huh? Champ it is, then."

Meredith kept up the one-sided conversation as she worked. "Wasn't it considerate of Stacy to take a long nap this morning so I could get this painting done? She's a good baby, Champ, despite that crying episode last night. You should have been there. The magnificent Lawyer Brooks didn't even know how to hold a baby. You'd have thought I was asking him to hold a vial of nitroglycerin. And then, suddenly, zip! Stacy quieted down and went right to sleep."

She shrugged her shoulders and dipped the brush into the can again. "Who can figure men or babies? They're even more unpredictable than cats.

"Do you have a home somewhere, or are you trying to mooch some food? Sorry, but I'm fresh out of cat food." She tensed, and her easy smile faded. *I'm damned lucky just to have people food again. We can thank the magnificent Lawyer Brooks for that, too.*

Once more she pondered the riddle of Kyle Sawyer Brooks, who held her in disdain, yet helped her; who seemed unapproachable yet allowed a priest to intimidate him into taking in a woman and her baby.

She finished her painting and took the brushes to the water spigot to clean them. Champ followed her.

He rubbed up against her legs until he stepped in a rivulet of water, then lifted his wet paw, shook it, and stalked off with his tail crooked into a high inverted *J*. Meredith laughed and went back to washing her brush. With luck, she'd be able to fix herself a sandwich and eat it at leisure before Stacy woke up.

She ate her sandwich in peace and cleared away the debris from lunch. She was debating between eating the last forkful of tuna salad or scraping it into the garbage disposal when she remembered Champ's hungry look and scraped the leftover dab into a plastic margarine container and took it outside. The cat waited until she'd put it down and walked a safe distance away before sauntering to the dish and devouring the tuna. Then he plopped down, wrapped his tail around his hind legs and meowed.

"You're welcome," Meredith said, walking over to pick up the container.

Champ meandered over and allowed her to pet him before striding off again. Meredith carried the bowl inside. By the time she'd rinsed it and put it in the dishwasher, Stacy was awake and bawling. Meredith carried her to the living room to nurse her.

"That's it, little one," Meredith said, her mother's heart swelling with love as Stacy suckled heartily. "Eat hearty. We've got a busy afternoon of shopping ahead. You're going to be a good girl for me, aren't you? All that fussing isn't going to be a daily routine, is it?"

Stacy paused for a moment to smack her lips and take a breath.

"That's it," Meredith said. "Play innocent. Pretend you'd never even think about being fussy. You little stinker. You think I'm going to forget you screamed your head off for six hours with me and then fell asleep on Lawyer Brooks's shoulder? I'm surprised the starch in his shirt didn't keep you awake."

Sighing, she let her head drop against the back of the chair. "I know. He's big and he's strong and he made you feel secure."

And whether I like him or not, he's the only security either of us has right now. I suppose a little gratitude would be in order.

"He wasn't so awful last night," she mused. "In fact, he was almost human. He was *concerned* about you, kiddo." She caressed Stacy's foot with her palm as she spoke. "He offered to take you to the clinic. He was actually kind of cute when I put you on his shoulder."

Meredith smiled at the memory. "You're too little to appreciate it, but there was a glint of sheer terror in his eyes!"

And what about later, after he'd put Stacy down— what kind of glint was in his eyes then?

Meredith's smile faded. *Don't flatter yourself. He wasn't thinking what you thought he was thinking. And if he was, it was a temporary aberration. You wouldn't want him thinking it anyway—any more than you want to admit that you were thinking it might be nice to have him take you in his arms and reassure you, the way he had Stacy.*

At last Stacy stopped nursing and smacked her lips, resting again. "Ready to try the other tap, kiddo?" Meredith asked, shifting her to the other breast. "You finish up, now, so we can get you all dressed up and run our errands."

And I can put these crazy thoughts about Kyle Sawyer Brooks out of my head.

MEREDITH WAS chopping pickles for a potato salad when Kyle arrived home that evening. He said hello, then routinely twisted a knob on the telephone answering machine.

Meredith looked up as she returned his hello. The knot of his tie had been loosened, the top button of his shirt unbuttoned, his coat removed and slung over his shoulder, where it hung suspended from two fingers of his left hand. He was at home, comfortable. She forced her eyes from the casual intimacy inherent in that loosened tie and the five-o'clock shadow of beard on his cheek that made her suddenly feel like an intruder in his house.

Seconds later a voice came through the speaker. "This is Dot, from Dot's Used Furniture." Meredith stopped her chopping to listen to the message. "I finally spoke to the boy who works at the store next door," Dot continued. "He can bring your furniture tomorrow afternoon about four, if that's okay. Please call me if it's not."

Kyle erased the message and reset the machine. "Did you get that?"

Meredith nodded without turning to face him. "Yes. That'll be perfect. The mattresses are supposed to get here tomorrow, too. Maybe I can get my quarters together by tomorrow night and vacate the guest room."

"Yes . . . well, there's no real hurry," Kyle said. Then, spying Stacy in her infant seat centered on the work island, he walked over to her. "She's okay today? No lingering effects from last night's crisis?"

"She slept well. In fact, she slept until almost nine, which is a record. She must have been exhausted from all the crying."

Kyle was staring at the baby, debating what to do about her. "You can talk to her or touch her," Meredith told him. "Babies like attention."

Kyle gave her a questioning look.

"Just say her name," she prompted.

"Stacy," Kyle said tentatively. He looked to Meredith for guidance.

Meredith rolled her eyes. "Try touching her hand. That's easy enough."

When he did so, Stacy captured his forefinger by wrapping her tiny hand around it. "She's got quite a grip," he observed, genuinely surprised.

Meredith had stopped her work and walked over to stand next to him, taking pleasure in his discovery of her daughter. "It's a reflex."

"She's staring at me," he observed.

"Babies love faces."

"Can she see—I mean, really see? Focus?"

"Sure," Meredith replied. "She's a human being, you know. She's just little."

"She resembles you."

"Do you think so?"

"Definitely. There's something about her mouth, and around the eyes." He turned to Meredith. "Will she have hair soon?"

Meredith laughed. "That takes a few months, depending on the baby."

"Does she look like Castor at all?"

Meredith stiffened. "Sometimes when she looks at me in a certain way, or moves her head at a certain angle, I see a resemblance. I try not to dwell on it."

But I'm glad Stacy is a girl. I'm glad she's not a boy who looks just like Thomas. I'm only human. I'm not sure I could have been as close to a miniature Thomas.

"I shouldn't have asked that," Kyle apologized. "I wasn't thinking."

"It's a logical question," she stated, purposely not looking at him.

"But it upset you."

"It's not exactly a tragedy that she looks a little like Thomas. He may be pond scum as a person, but he's pretty." She went back to the cutting board and scraped the pickles into the bowl with the boiled potatoes. Centering an onion on the board, she halved it with a savage chop. "He's Stacy's father. Nothing is ever going to change that fact."

She continued slicing the onion. The sharp vapors brought tears to her eyes.

"Strong onion," Kyle commented. She nodded.

"What's this?" he asked, pointing to a bowl of marinating chunks of beef.

"Shish kebabs—or it will be. I saw the grill on the patio, but I can broil them in the oven if you don't want to cook outside."

"I'll crank up the grill," he offered. "Just let me get out of this suit."

She had the potato salad in the refrigerator by the time he'd dressed and returned to the kitchen. She held up a skewer. "I don't know which vegetables you like, so you'll have to tell me what to put on your vegetable kebab."

"What have we got?"

"Everything but mushrooms," Meredith said.

Later, as they ate, Kyle remarked, "I saw the headboard outside. It looks good."

"It should be almost dry. Stacy was a perfect angel today and I was able to get the second coat on this afternoon. Which reminds me, I'll need a screwdriver if you have one."

"A screwdriver?"

"To put the bed together. I was hoping that the people who deliver the mattresses can put them right on the frame."

"I'll put it together for you when we finish eating."

"It's probably not dry enough to handle."

"Then I'll put it together in the morning. It shouldn't take more than a few minutes."

Meredith started to protest but thought better of the idea. "I'm too tired to turn down help," she said.

He scrutinized her face carefully. "You do look tired."

"Busy day," she explained, dismissing his concern.

"You're trying to do too much."

How long did it take a woman to regain her strength after childbirth? Especially a woman who'd been living in a car and not eating properly?

"I'll be fine after a good night's sleep."

"Get one," Kyle told her. "That's an order. I'd hate to have you collapse on me."

"That would be inconvenient, I'm sure."

"Don't mock my concern, Meredith. As your employer, I'm responsible for your welfare."

His words hung in the air, sounding stiff and formal and official—none of which was compatible with genuine concern.

Why? Meredith wondered. *What made you hire me, when it's obvious you'd rather not have the aggravation?*

The prolonged, painful silence finally became so oppressive that Meredith heaved a sigh of relief when Stacy began fussing. She excused herself and carried Stacy into the living room, speaking soothingly to her.

Kyle finished his meal alone, and felt every minute of his solitary state as though it were a punishment. He wasn't sure what annoyed him more: being stuck with an impossible woman, or inadvertently offending her every time they engaged in the most innocuous conversations. In almost every exchange with her, he ended up either defensive or apologetic—or worse, both.

What had he said that was so awful? The stubborn fool *was* trying to do too much. He'd just expressed a little human concern, and her hackles had gone up faster than a hound's on a coon trail.

What did she want from him? He'd given her a home, a job; he was handling her suit against Castor. He'd even held her baby, for God's sake, which was something he'd never allowed himself to be suckered into before by anyone—relative, clients or friends. He'd been nice to her, damn it. Generous. Charming to a fault. Polite beyond all reasonable minimum standards of behavior.

But there had been censure in the way she'd excused herself from the table and rebuff in the set of her narrow shoulders as she walked out of the room. He shoved his chair away from the table and strode to the living room, then paused in the arched doorway, trying to decide whether he should apologize or pretend the awkward moments at the table had never happened.

Stacy was stretched out in her mother's lap. Meredith's head was bowed over her daughter's face. Her obliviousness to his presence stung like a calculated rejection. Kyle knew he should slip away and not disturb her communion with the baby, but spoke her name instead. She looked up at him, surprised by his presence. Kyle's breath caught in his throat when he saw the glisten of tears on her cheeks. Had he hurt her that much? He said her name again, turning it into a question.

"She smiled," Meredith said softly.

"The baby?"

Meredith nodded. "I knew it was time, and I've been waiting, but I never expected..." A fresh tear slid down her cheek. "I never expected it to be so beautiful."

Kyle sat down next to her on the sofa. A sense of wonder overwhelmed him as he, too, stared at Stacy's face. How could anything so tiny generate so much emotion and excitement?

"Is smiling something they have to learn?" he asked. "I would have thought it was instinctive."

"It's . . . They have to reach a certain point of readiness. Sometimes they seem to be smiling, but it's not a conscious thing, just an involuntary grimace. Voluntary smiling—smiling because she's happy—is different."

Meredith bent forward, putting her face close to Stacy's. "Hey, Stacy. Sweetheart, why don't you smile at Mama again? Show us how pretty you are when you smile."

With a little more coaxing, Stacy did as she was asked.

Kyle was awed by the transformation in the tiny face. The baby's smile expressed such innocent pleasure. Her mouth opened as her lips turned upward, her cheeks plumped, her eyes lit up.

"It's as though a light bulb came on inside her," Kyle whispered to Meredith, who nodded in agreement.

For a full minute they sat there coaxing Stacy to smile and reveling in the miracle of her new achievement. Kyle stretched his arm across Meredith's shoulders, not immediately cognizant of the fact that he was sharing with her a moment so special and private that it was usually reserved for parents only. Then Meredith turned her head and looked at him full face, and the color that rose in her cheeks as she forgot what she had been about to say made him suddenly aware of the intimacy of the way he was touching her.

Embarrassed, he withdrew his arm and straightened his spine, putting a buffer of space between them.

"I'd better get started on the dishes," Meredith announced, lifting Stacy to her shoulder and standing. "Stacy'll be howling for her beddy-bye snack in a little while."

"I'm going to catch the news," Kyle said, reaching for the remote control for the television.

When the news was over he ventured into the kitchen, where Meredith was giving the counters a final wipe down. He walked to the desk, where he'd left his portfolio. "I brought home some papers for you to fill out," he told her.

Meredith stopped her work in midswipe. "What kind of papers?"

"I drew up a list of questions. I need some general background information about you and Castor."

"I told you everything."

"You gave me the big picture. I need details. If Castor decides to fight you on the support suit, his attorney will do a background check on you. I'd like to be one step ahead of him. If something comes up gray, I'd like to be prepared."

"'Gray'?"

"Anything that could be misconstrued if presented in the wrong way. We need to anticipate anything that might come up."

"I answered all your prying questions. There's nothing *gray* in my background."

"You can take my help or leave it," he said finally. "But if you take it, you take it all the way. I'll handle the case *pro bono publico*, but I won't handle it any differently than any other. Don't ask me to be a mediocre attorney."

He tossed the paper-clipped stack of papers onto the table. "It's your call. Either you cooperate and we do it right, or we don't do it."

Meredith slapped the dishcloth into the sink, rinsed her hands and stalked to the table, scowling at Kyle as she brushed past him. She sat down and pulled the papers in front of her.

Kyle sat down opposite her, and was unnerved to see an enigmatic smile play at her mouth as she read. "What's the joke?" he asked.

"The questions are typed."

"I had my secretary transcribe them."

"Of course."

"I don't know why you find that humorous."

Meredith was quiet a moment. "You're very thorough, aren't you?"

"It's one of the things that makes me very good."

Modest, too, Meredith thought sarcastically. "I need a pen," she told him, turning her attention back to the papers in front of her.

Kyle handed her one from his briefcase—a gold-plated ballpoint. Meredith took it self-consciously and began writing. "Do you actually expect me to remember half of this stuff?"

"Just fill in what you can. Phone numbers and zip codes are easy to find."

Alternating between furious scribbling and scowlful thought, Meredith finally worked her way through the stack. "What's this one?" she asked about the bottom page. "It's different from the others."

"Oh. That's my official client-information form. Strictly routine."

"You have a lot of routines," Meredith grumbled.

"That's another of the things that make me good," Kyle drolly countered.

Stacy, who'd been fretting halfheartedly for a minute or two, finally let out a genuine cry of outrage. Meredith laid Kyle's pen atop the papers and shoved them in his direction. "Finished in the nick of time."

She lifted Stacy from the infant seat, murmuring re-assurances, then looked at Kyle. "I'm sorry if I seemed uncooperative," she told him. "I just . . . This entire legal thing is so . . . unpleasant."

Kyle stood and capped her shoulder with his long fingers in a comforting way. "I know it's difficult having your past put under a magnifying glass."

Meredith tucked her chin against Stacy's head, partly to comfort the child, but also to avoid eye contact with Kyle.

"Castor may be reasonable and agree to the support without a fight," Kyle said, and felt the slight movement of Meredith's shoulder under his hand as she shrugged, indicating her lack of faith in Castor's good sense or easy acquiescence.

Stacy was nuzzling against Meredith's chest, searching for food; finding only cotton knit, she wailed in frustration. Meredith rolled her eyes at Kyle. "I've got to feed her before she gets too upset."

Kyle nodded. "Good night."

Her "Good night" was muffled by the baby's cries. Kyle trailed her as far as the living room and turned the television back on, but he found it difficult to concentrate on the program with the cries of the baby filtering through the closed guest-room door.

He found it even more difficult to concentrate when the crying ceased. He kept imagining Meredith holding Stacy, feeding her, speaking soothingly to her. He remembered the sweetness of Stacy's face when she smiled, and puzzled over its effect on him. What was it about this woman, and this child, that reached inside him to depths long untouched?

Is this what Mark had hoped for by forcing this gesture of Christian charity upon him? To shake him out of the complacency of his life? What right did any man—even a priest—have to foist responsibility for one human being—or two human beings, for that matter—onto another? What right did Mark have to force him to feel again, when he'd been managing quite well on zealously rationed emotions for so long? Wasn't it enough that he helped his clients? Did he have to get *involved*—and with a *charity* case?

Kyle had installed dam gates on his emotions years before. Through dogged determination and a strong survival instinct, he had always been able to harness his strong feelings before he became vulnerable.

Vulnerable. Kyle knew about vulnerability. Vulnerability united with guilt and pain was a dangerous force, destined to defeat a man who opened himself to caring.

His clients—all those women who'd been abused or ignored or abandoned or betrayed—wrung their hands and sobbed and told him how understanding he was. Kyle understood, all right. He understood that they were hurt because they'd *let* themselves be hurt; by caring, by loving, by giving of themselves, they'd set themselves up for abuse and betrayal and abandonment.

They considered him a helper, a defender of rights. But in reality, he was not a defender so much as an avenger. He worked through the justice system to legally assign blame and exact retribution. He meted out punishment to bullies and abusers and neglecters and philanderers—punishing them with the realization of their greatest fears: public disclosure, loss of esteem, stiff financial terms.

Kyle was effective because he understood fear as well as vulnerability. He was intimately acquainted with the fear of disclosure because he held within himself his own awful secret—an ugliness incompatible with his sleek, impeccable image. He lived with the fear that someone would discover that the compassionate Kyle Brooks, champion of abused and betrayed women, was actually just a veneer disguising a mass of shame and guilt.

Kyle lived within parameters of emotional investment that never required him to delve deeply enough inside himself for anything that might touch that guilt. He functioned efficiently with tunnel-vision determination. By focusing on getting the job done, he kept his mind diverted. He couldn't forget the guilt, but he could ignore it—as long as he didn't care too much. When he began caring, he reawakened the guilt, as well.

He tried to concentrate on the television program, a weekly drama series that followed attorneys from boardroom to courtroom to bedroom, but found it dull. He'd marveled at a baby's smile, and now the contrast between the innocence of that smile and the ugliness of his own dark secret tormented him.

8

"IT'S *NOT* WORKING OUT, thank you very much for asking," Kyle said into the telephone receiver. Mark had some nerve, calling and nonchalantly inquiring how his new housekeeper was working out.

"What's the problem?" Mark asked in a nauseatingly cheerful voice.

Kyle complained. "It's just an impossible situation."

"There has to be something specific if it's that impossible," Mark replied—so calmly that Kyle wished he could crawl through the phone lines and throttle him.

"All right. I'll be specific. It's Meredith. She's impossible."

"She isn't doing her job?"

"She's *doing it!*" Kyle retorted, sounding as if he were accusing Meredith of doing some nefarious deed. "That's just the point."

"I'm a priest, not a psychic. Want to explain that one to me?"

"She's just..." Kyle grumbled, disgusted at not being able to put his objections into words. "She bakes cinnamon oatmeal muffins for breakfast."

"So?"

Dead silence. Finally Mark persisted by asking, "Are they edible?"

"They're delicious. Everything she cooks is delicious."

"I can see where that could be traumatic," Mark responded wryly.

"It's not just the cooking," Kyle went on, his agitation growing. "She put a basket of dried flower petals in the bathroom to make it smell fresh."

"Does it smell bad?"

"No. It's okay. It's just . . . Damn it! She's invading my space. She's crowding me."

"Does she nag you? Make you wipe your shoes at the door?"

"No."

"Steal the grocery money? Tipple liquor from your bar?"

"Get serious, Mark. She doesn't do anything like that. She just . . . cooks and cleans and makes sure the towels match."

"Excuse me, but isn't that what a housekeeper is supposed to do?"

"You don't understand," Kyle said. "She's too damned . . . efficient. I told her to furnish the maid's quarters—you know, go out, buy some furniture, something to cover the windows. Does she go to Ethan Allen or Windows-R-Us? Hell, no. She's out buying used furniture and painting it. She's got her sewing machine set up on a card table and she's making curtains out of some sheets she found at a clearance sale."

"Sounds like a handy woman to have around."

"She's nesting, Mark. It's as plain as day. She bought a rocking chair to rock the baby in, and she's making cushions for it that match the curtains."

"She's probably grateful to have a roof over her head."

"You still don't get it, do you?" Kyle complained. "She had me hanging blinds night before last. Hanging blinds! I thought she'd have someone come in and install them, but she gushed on and on about how lucky it was that the window was a standard size and she was able to find prefab instead of having to order them custom."

"Now, there's a reason to kick her back out into the streets."

"She made fun of my screwdriver. The automatic one. The kind that sits on a base recharging when you're not using it. She seemed to think it amusing that someone would have a screwdriver that turned by itself."

"Some women have no respect for the things a man holds most sacred."

"Don't you start on me, too," Kyle warned. "It was a gift from a client who owned a chain of hardware stores. I never used the damned thing until Ms. Fix-It-Up moved in."

A silence ensued. Finally, Kyle challenged, "Well?"

"I think you should fire her."

"You can't be serious."

"You hold all the cards, Kyle. If she's making your life that miserable, there's no reason you should put up with the aggravation."

"But she wouldn't have anywhere else to go. She'd be back living in her car again."

"Sure. But that's not your problem."

Kyle burst out with a blistering expletive. "You know damned well she's my problem. You dropped her and her baby squarely in my lap."

"Ah...yes. The baby—how *is* the baby? Still sweet?"

"She's . . ." Kyle hesitated. "What do I know about babies?"

"You're living in the same house with one. I should think you'd know something about her health and welfare. She's healthy, isn't she?"

"I suppose so. She doesn't seem to be sick or anything." There was another hesitation. Kyle shifted uncomfortably in his chair. "She smiles a lot. She just learned how a few days ago, and now she smiles all the time. Meredith makes a big deal about it."

"Most mothers do."

"Yes. Well...most mothers aren't living in my house."

"What's really bothering you?" Mark asked.

"I don't like . . . I like simplicity, and she's . . ."

After a very long pause, Mark prompted, "She's?"

"She's complicated. She makes everything complicated."

"Good for her," Mark replied. "It's about time someone complicated your life a little."

THE FIRST THING Kyle noticed when he got out of his car was the orange tabby that had been hanging around. He took several steps toward it, thinking the stray would scurry off, as usual; but the cat didn't budge. Plopped on his fat behind near the patio door, he held his ground, smugly munching away at something.

Oh, great. He's killed a bird, Kyle thought, but a closer check revealed a brightly colored plastic pet dish filled with what looked like breakfast cereal. The cat paused in his gluttonous pursuit of gastronomical delight long enough to cast a wary glance at Kyle, then meowed haughtily before resuming his meal.

Pompous feline! Kyle bent to pick up a piece of whatever was in the bowl and smell it. Definitely fishy. Cat food.

Cat food! This was the last straw—the one that broke the camel's back. He could take little baskets of pot-pourri in the bathroom and having his screwdriver ridiculed after he was rooked into manual labor, but he did not—*did not*—have to tolerate an obnoxious cat.

He stalked to the side door through which he always entered the house and yanked it open. The aroma of something Italian and delicious-smelling greeted him, and his mouth watered in anticipation. That automatic response annoyed him. He wasn't going to be diverted by something that smelled as if it had been put together by angels. He'd said the first half of Meredith's name when she stepped into view from the direction of the laundry room.

"Hi!" she greeted, smiling.

"There's a stray cat next to the patio eating cat food," he roared.

Meredith's smile faded. "That's Champ."

"My God, you've named him."

"He looks like a Champ," Meredith explained lamely.

"What he looks like," Kyle said, "is a fat-assed flea-ridden, scruffy-coated stray cat."

"I don't think he has fleas. I haven't noticed him scratching."

"You gave him cat food, didn't you?"

Her eyes turned a deeper shade of gray. "He was hungry!"

Dead silence ensued, during which Kyle tried not to notice the pain in the depths of those gray eyes, tried not to read her mind and follow the obvious track of her reasoning to the parallel between herself and the cat.

Oh, no, he thought. *You're not going to squirm out of this one with the sympathy factor.*

"Don't you like cats?"

"Not stray cats that hang out at my house."

"He's very tame."

"I am not running a soup kitchen for indigent tom-cats!"

Meredith looked stricken. "Only for indigent peo-ple. Is that it?"

"Don't put words in my mouth."

"I didn't have to."

"There's no correlation at all."

"Isn't there?"

Meredith's chest rose and fell as she struggled to contain her anger while they glared at each other.

"Why?" she asked, at last giving voice to the ques-tion that had plagued her ever since she'd gotten into the car with him that first night and had recognized his resentment over being stuck with her. "Why did you agree to take Stacy and me in, when you clearly don't want us here?"

"I was planning on hiring a housekeeper," he replied after a long pause.

"Not a homeless one. Not an *indigent* woman with a child." She gave the word an ugly inflection and Kyle flinched. "It was your word," she said.

"I was talking about the cat."

"Were you?"

He didn't answer and Meredith shuddered. "I hate that word. I hate the sound of it." Raising her eyes to Kyle's face, she challenged, "Do you know how people look at you when you go into a hospital as an indigent? It's as though you're a different species from other peo-ple, as though your body works differently. If they had a zoo for people, they'd have different cages and dif-ferent signs for them. The Indigents and the Solvents."

Meredith walked to the stove and lifted the lid of the Dutch oven, then stirred the sauce simmering in the pot. Wooden spoon in hand, she turned back to Kyle. "I saved the grocery receipt," she told him. "You can take the price of the cat food and the bowl out of my salary."

"Damn it!" Kyle fired back. "It's not the money. It's . . . don't you realize that by feeding that mangy cat—"

"He doesn't have mange."

"By feeding him on my property, you're assuming the presumption of ownership. You're making me legally liable for anything that cat does."

"Legally liable?" Meredith asked incredulously, slapping the spoon onto the counter. "That's lawyer talk. Lawyer thinking. Everybody has cats."

"If that miniature tiger went three houses down and scratched some child—or someone's expensive car, for that matter— I could get the pants sued off me."

"Let them sue me, instead," she said. "If I'm buying the food, then technically it's my cat."

"You have more important things to do with your money than feed freeloading tomcats."

"Like saving it so I can move out as soon as I can get a real job?"

"You have a job!"

"I may have been homeless, I may be indigent, but I'm not stupid!" she retorted.

Words of reassurance stuck in Kyle's throat. *Had he expected her to be stupid because she'd been homeless?* He suppressed the question, not liking what the answer would tell him about himself.

"I know Father Mark pressured you into taking us in. I know you don't want us here, and I plan to leave as soon as I—"

Tears glossed her eyes and she dropped her head, unable to face him. When she spoke her voice was strained. "I don't have anyplace else to go right now. I can't make Stacy live in the car again if there's any alternative at all."

Kyle fought back the wave of compassion he felt for her, concentrating instead on the need to remain objective and dispassionate toward her. *Pro bono* or not, she was a client, and like most of his clients, she needed his services because she'd been foolish and failed to protect her rights. She was in trouble because she'd trusted the wrong man and, having seen his true colors, had failed to assert herself and demand that he live up to his moral obligations. She was not only foolish, but weak, and he had little respect for weak, foolish people.

Still, as he looked at her, trying fiercely to muster disdain for her, he sensed a strength in her, an innate dignity that had survived the humiliation of homelessness. While he searched inside himself for disdain, he found respect in its stead—respect for that resilient dignity, for the tenacious way she clung to hope and optimism.

He fought his urge to comfort her—but fought and lost.

Meredith struggled, too—against her own need for human comfort and reassurance. She just *had* to be strong.

But she faltered and took one small step forward—a tiny step that brought her into the circle of Kyle's arms. As his strong arms enfolded her, soothed and consoled her, she sighed against his broad, firm chest and relaxed against the length of his body. She slid her arms around his waist, wanting more consolation, more reassurance, more sensation of human contact.

Arms entwined and bodies aligned, they remained in a silent embrace for several long moments. The solidity and voluptuousness of Meredith's body, a tactile contrast to the impression of fragility she radiated, surprised Kyle. It surprised him, too, how comforted he felt by those full, feminine curves when he'd thought it was he who would be doing the comforting.

"You don't have to be in a hurry to go anywhere," he told her. "You're doing a good job with the house. I'm . . . if I seem aloof, it's just that I'm used to living alone, and it's difficult for me to get used to having another person around."

Meredith nodded slowly, her cheek brushing against his chest. It would have been easy to stay there next to his warm, lulling strength, but she eased away, pulling out of his embrace, before the luxury of human comfort became too irresistible. It had been a momentary lapse of—two human beings consoling each other, that's all. That was all either of them could allow it to be, Meredith acknowledged.

"I hope you like old-fashioned spaghetti and meat balls," she said, lifting the pot lid so she could give the sauce another stir.

The thick tension had dissipated. "If that tastes as good as it smells, I'm going to have to give you a raise," Kyle remarked as he jauntily picked up his suit jacket, flipped it over his shoulder and left the room. He didn't excuse himself as he headed for the back of the house. His daily routine of changing clothes soon after arriving home from work was well established.

Meredith filled a large saucepan with water and started it heating so she could cook the spaghetti. She was slicing Italian bread for garlic toast when she heard Stacy stirring. Rolling her eyes over Stacy's bad timing, she turned off the burner under the water and dashed to her quarters, where Stacy was crying impatiently for a feeding and a fresh diaper.

When she returned to the kitchen, Kyle was standing at the butcher-block island thumbing through her high-school yearbook.

"I meant to put that away," she said. "It was packed with my cookbooks." The cookbooks—a respectable collection—were lined up on the counter between two heavy crockery vases filled with wooden cooking utensils.

Kyle looked up. "You don't mind, do you?"

Meredith shrugged. "No. But I can't figure out what you'd find interesting about an old yearbook."

"Faces," Kyle replied. He tapped Meredith's senior-class picture with his forefinger. "Or one face in particular."

"It's just an old photograph."

"You look so young and bright-eyed," Kyle remarked.

"Maybe I was, then," Meredith said. After considering the comment, she added, "Sometimes I forget I was ever young."

"That's a harsh statement for a twenty-three-year-old."

"I haven't felt young in a very long time." She was holding Stacy, and tilted her head forward to drop a kiss on her scalp before lowering her into her infant seat.

"I hired an investigator to do a background check once and he sent me photocopies of pages from a high-school yearbook. He said you could find out a lot about a person in a yearbook."

Meredith turned on the burner under the saucepan. "Dinner should be ready in about fifteen minutes."

"'Student Council vice president,'" Kyle read. "Gourmet Society—I didn't know high schools *had* gourmet societies."

"My home-ec teacher organized it. We used to plan seven-course dinners and cater events for parents or teachers."

"So that's where you learned to cook."

Meredith gave him a sharp look. "It's where I learned to cook *fancy*. I learned the basics from my mother."

"You've never mentioned your mother before."

"She died." Meredith's taut voice revealed raw pain.

Equally raw pain crossed over Kyle's face. "I'm sorry."

Meredith walked to the stove and checked the saucepan to see if the water was boiling. But a slight tremble in her shoulders betrayed her reaction to his expression of sympathy before she picked up the box of spaghetti and broke the noodles in half, then plunged them into the water. She did not turn back to him immediately, but deliberately busied herself stirring the sauce and preparing the garlic bread.

"You were in the National Honor Society," Kyle noted.

Meredith stopped her work. "That was a long time ago."

"You're twenty-three, Meredith. How long ago could it have been?"

"A lifetime ago."

Kyle looked from the carefree teenager in the senior portrait to the sad gray eyes of the woman in front of him. "What happened to you?"

"Life," she replied. "And death."

Again Kyle flinched at the mention of death. "Your mother?"

"Yes."

"Was it sudden?"

For a horrible second, he feared she might burst into tears. But she managed to remain stoic. "Her illness was sudden. Her death wasn't."

"That must have been difficult for you."

"I had thought . . . it was awful when my father died. Everything changed then, too, but at least then, my mother and I had each other."

"How old were you when your father—"

"Died!" she asked, when Kyle stumbled over the word. "Eleven. It was a construction accident. He fell. It was quite sudden." She grew thoughtfully quiet. "I didn't know then that a sudden death can be a blessing."

"No!" Kyle objected. "There should be time to say what needs to be said, time to prepare—"

"You lost someone, too," Meredith guessed.

His expression grew guarded and closed. He was saved from having to reply when the saucepan boiled over, and the water steamed and hissed as it landed on the hot burner.

"Damn!" Meredith exclaimed, dashing to the stove to lift the pot from the burner, turn down the heat, and pour off some of the water. "I'm not used to this cookware or these burners yet," she said defensively.

"No one can say you can't boil water," Kyle teased. "You just have a slight problem keeping it in the pot."

Relieved by his humorous remark, Meredith teased back, "It's not good policy to harass the cook—you never know what might turn up on your plate!"

"No complaints, so far."

"You never know, though. I might get miffed and sneak in a . . ." She paused for effect. "A . . ."

"You don't mean," Kyle said, affecting horror-movie drama. "You couldn't be referring to—"

"Yes!" she confirmed. "The dreaded fungus! A *mushroom*."

Unexpectedly, Stacy let out a whimpering cry.

"See," Kyle told her. "Your daughter doesn't like them, either."

Stacy continued fretting and, with a quick glance to make sure the spaghetti didn't need attention, Meredith unstrapped her from the infant seat, then nestled her on her shoulder. "She probably has a bubble."

"What's a bubble?"

"Sometimes babies swallow air when they're feeding, and they get uncomfortable. That's why mothers do what is commonly referred to as 'burping.'"

She patted Stacy's back rhythmically to demonstrate. At length her efforts were rewarded with a hefty burp from Stacy. "There now, that's better, isn't it?" To Kyle, she said, "See. It has nothing to do with mushrooms!"

Stacy cooed happily and smiled at her mother—until Meredith tried to put her back into the infant seat and she rebelled. "Stacy, please. Mommy needs to fix dinner. The noodles are going to get soggy."

Stacy continued to fret. Meredith sighed in exasperation as she reached for the straps to fasten Stacy into the seat. "You're just going to be fussy this time of day, aren't you? I thought after that long nap—"

"I'll hold her," Kyle offered.

"Are you sure?"

"We wouldn't want soggy spaghetti, would we?"

Meredith scooped Stacy up and put her in Kyle's lap. "It's worth a try."

Kyle positioned the baby so that she could see Meredith, and she quieted down.

"You're getting pretty good at holding her," Meredith commented as she drained the pasta.

"Nothing to it," Kyle said, letting Stacy grasp his forefinger in her tiny fist. "I think she's getting used to me."

"Umm," Meredith agreed absently. Stacy *was* getting used to Kyle. In fact, since that night when she'd cozied up in his arms and fallen asleep after her fit of colic, she seemed at ease with him. It was natural, Meredith supposed, since he was the only human being besides Meredith that Stacy saw with any regularity. It was probably good for Stacy to have daily exchanges with a man, too, since she had no contact with her father.

Still, Meredith had doubts about the wisdom of letting Stacy bond with Kyle when his role in her life was destined to be temporary.

Should she deliberately discourage him from holding Stacy, so her baby wouldn't miss him when they moved out on their own? Or should she encourage it, so Stacy wouldn't be wary of men when she was older?

Impossible questions. The riddles of motherhood. Seized with trepidation, Meredith shivered. *If it's this complicated now, what will it be like when Stacy's old enough to ask me why she doesn't have a daddy like all the other kids?*

She dumped the spaghetti into a serving bowl and carried it to the table. *No one ever said motherhood would be easy.*

When the entire meal was on the table, she took Stacy from Kyle's lap. "Okay, kiddo, it's into the seat again for you."

Stacy sat quietly, watching them eat during the pleasant, unhurried dinner. When they'd finished eating, Kyle complimented Meredith on the delicious meal. Then, excusing himself, he carried his briefcase into the dining room to go over some legal documents he'd brought home from the office.

Meredith was just finishing in the kitchen when he walked back in, carrying a check. "Tomorrow's the fifteenth," he told her, laying it on the work island near Stacy's infant seat.

Her first paycheck! Meredith had to control an urge to dash to it, pick it up, read the numbers. Instead, she said softly, "Thank you."

"I guess you have big plans for your afternoon off."

"Just some shopping."

Awkwardly, Meredith continued, "I've bought some personal items for Stacy and me along with the groceries. I've been compiling a list. I meant to give it to you so you could deduct the expenses from my salary."

Kyle sighed. Since he had plenty of money, it meant less to him than to her. If she hadn't been so serious, he would have told her not to worry about the extra items. But since it was an issue of pride that she took from him only what she earned, he held back and reassured her, instead.

"Keep that list until the end of the month. I'm sure there are other things you need that you've been holding off buying, and the next check will be bigger."

She nodded mutely, silently thanking him for letting her maintain her dignity through her small display of self-sufficiency.

Kyle spoke her name hesitantly. Her gaze still locked with his, Meredith cocked her head.

"About the cat," he said.

"I'm sorry," she replied. "I should have talked to you about it first. I...he was friendly and hungry, and I like cats and it didn't occur to me you'd mind."

Kyle hesitated. "You can keep the damned cat."

"You're not afraid you'll be sued?"

He frowned. "What's life without risk?"

Meredith smiled beatifically, and her eyes grew suspiciously bright. Impulsively she reached up to cradle Kyle's face in her hands, and stood on tiptoe to kiss his cheek. "Thank you."

Kyle choked back an expletive and restrained himself from turning her gesture of appreciation into more than it was. He reluctantly noted that she had a lovely smile. "If you ever get that mangy beast to the point where he'll ride in a car without ripping it apart," he told her, "I'd appreciate it if you'd go have him vaccinated for rabies. The vet bill's on me."

9

SELDOM had a few ounces felt more like a few tons.

Meredith looked at her reflection in the oversize mirror of the salon and felt as though a great weight had been taken off her shoulders. Actually, she had just treated herself to a beauty-salon shampoo and cut—all for under ten dollars at a chain renowned for economical service.

Thick and full-bodied, her hair was neither too straight nor too curly, too fine or too coarse. But even the best hair demanded a good cut now and again, and she had neglected hers for longer than she cared to admit. Her bangs had grown to midcheek; and the rest of her hair, from jawline to shoulder length. Now the excess lay on the salon floor.

As she left the shop Meredith gave her head a toss, feeling lighter, cleaner, younger and prettier than she had since leaving Indiana—since Thomas had insultingly rejected her and refused to take on responsibility for their child, since she'd gone through pregnancy and childbirth alone, since she'd been evicted from her home and forced to live in her car.

She paused outside the salon, considering how to spend the rest of the afternoon. Stacy had been a good sport about shopping and was asleep now, but undoubtedly she would soon wake up hungry, and *vocal*. Meredith decided not to push her luck too far and was walking to the car when she spied the video store next door to the salon. On impulse, she went inside and browsed through the movies for rent. Kyle had said she could use the VCR anytime she liked; it would be nice to sit back and watch a movie. She would drop by the supermarket for popcorn—it wasn't exactly most people's idea of a party-hearty, but it would be a pleasant break from routine.

KYLE HADN'T PLANNED on going home immediately after work. Since it was Meredith's day off, he had thought he might go out with some of his fellow attorneys for dinner. But since nothing had panned out, he'd decided to go home for a change of clothes before heading out for fast food. As he maneuvered through the thick traffic on Interstate 4, he looked forward to being home alone again—like old times, with no one expecting him to hang blinds, or looking at him with sad eyes when he asked why she was feeding a stray cat. It might be a good night just to sprawl on the couch and vegetate, enjoy the solitude while he had the chance.

He was chagrined to see Meredith's car when he turned into the driveway—chagrined, but not disappointed. Why should he be surprised? After all, how long could a woman shop with an infant in tow? And where else would she have gone? To see her old boss, the one who wouldn't let her work when she'd needed to make money? To visit the friend with the lecherous live-in boyfriend? To see Castor? Heaven forbid!

No wonder the woman took in stray cats!

Meredith was sitting on the sofa, with Stacy nestled in her lap, engrossed in something on television and didn't see Kyle until he was well into the room.

"I didn't hear you come in," she said, turning off the VCR with the remote control.

"Whatever you're watching must be good."

Guiltily she looked over at him. "It's a movie. You said I could use the VCR."

"Sure. Anytime. What are you watching?"

"I rented a couple of movies," she replied, naming a recent cop movie that had just been released in video.

"I've heard that's good," Kyle remarked, crossing the room on the way to his bedroom. "Sorry I disturbed you."

After changing clothes he returned to the living room. Meredith was as engrossed as ever in the television screen, but it was no cop movie she was watching.

"Is that *Bambi?*" Kyle asked incredulously.

"Shh!" Meredith held up her hand to halt his words. "They're going back into the meadow."

"I haven't seen this since I was a kid," Kyle whispered, joining her on the sofa. There was a bowl of popcorn on the coffee table and he scooped up a handful.

"This is where the hunters—" Meredith gasped at the sound of a rifle firing. Bambi's pitiful cries for his mother brought tears to her eyes, and Bambi's father's proclamation that Bambi's mother wouldn't be coming back sent them trailing down her cheeks.

"Please don't cry," Kyle said.

Meredith sniffed. "I don't usually—"

"I can't bear to see a woman cry."

"I'm sorry. I—"

"Shh," he soothed, reaching out to wipe away her tears with his thumbs. The intimacy of his gesture shocked both of them, and they froze. Meredith wanted to say something, but nothing seemed appropriate.

After what felt like an eternity, Stacy made a gurgling sound and Meredith used the diversion to break her gaze away from Kyle's. She jiggled her arm gently until Stacy quieted, then sighed. "It's silly, isn't it, crying over a cartoon?"

"It's not just the movie, is it?"

She shook her head. "It's losing my mother . . . and being a mother and realizing how vulnerable children are." She looked down at Stacy, and her eyes grew bright again. "She's so little and needs so much."

"You take good care of her."

"I don't know what I'd do if I lost her. That's why . . . I was afraid they'd take her away from me if I went to the authorities for help. I was afraid they'd say I was incapable of supporting her."

She fell silent and an unexpected smile claimed her face as she became absorbed in the movie, again. "Look. Flower's falling in love."

Flower, then Thumper, and finally, Bambi, succumbed to the spell of springtime and first love. Kyle was surprised to realize he was laughing aloud at Bambi's shyness and Feline's precociousness; he was even more shocked to discover himself reaching for Meredith's hand when she sat tense and rigid while the characters fled the inferno of the forest fire. She gripped his fingers with near-painful pressure, gradually relaxing her grip when she saw the characters gather in the aftermath of the fire. They were holding hands in a gentle touch by the time Bambi's fawn appeared on the screen in the last scene.

As the credits rolled, Meredith drew her hand away abruptly, and picked up the remote control to stop and rewind the film. Kyle helped himself to some more popcorn. "This is delicious."

"Cholesterol city," Meredith said. "They had real butter on sale."

Kyle studied her face for a moment. It looked fuller, her features more voluptuous. Pretty. Since she'd been getting rest and balanced meals at his house, the gauntness in her cheeks and dark circles under her eyes had been gradually disappearing. This, however, was a dramatic change. "You've done something different with your hair," he observed.

Instinctively she raised her hand to pat the new hairdo. "I had it cut."

"It becomes you."

"Thank you."

She was dressed differently, too—in a softly pleated buff-colored skirt and a loose, pale blue blouse that made her skin look warm and velvety. Suddenly the factors clicked in Kyle's mind: the feminine clothes, the visit to the beauty shop, the first paycheck. She was indulging herself, celebrating. He felt pride in her.

"How about dinner?" he asked.

Caught off guard, she hesitated. "I didn't plan anything, but there's spaghetti sauce from last night. We could cook some noodles—"

He chuckled. "Not on your evening off. Let's go out."

"But Stacy—"

"We'll take her with us. People take babies into restaurants all the time."

"But we shouldn't—"

"Go out to dinner together? Why?"

"It's just not a good idea."

"What is this, reverse snobbery? You can't be seen with your boss?"

"I can't let you—"

"Of course, you can. You've got a new hairdo and you're all dressed up. Let's go celebrate."

"It's not a new hairdo. This is the way I usually wear my hair. It had just . . . It grew like crazy when I was pregnant and got shaggy. And I'm not dressed up. I just decided to try on some of my clothes to see if I could get into them, and these fit."

"Steak or seafood?"

"Kyle!"

"I'll tell you what, we'll wager."

"Bet?"

"You got it. You're a gourmet, right?"

Her eyes narrowed suspiciously. "Yes. Sort of."

"I'll bet you that I can take you out to eat something you've never eaten before."

"I doubt that."

"All right. We'll go to dinner, and if you've never eaten what I order for you, then dinner's on me. If you *have* eaten it before, I'll take the price of the meal out of your next check."

"You're on," she agreed. "As long as it's not monkey's brains or goat's eyes."

Kyle laughed. "Don't worry. I'm too much of a meat-and-potatoes man to subject you to anything that exotic."

BARNACLE PETE'S was a wooden structure built to resemble a fishing boat. "I've already tried squid-ink pasta," Meredith said, as they walked up the gangplank. "In fact, I know how to make it."

"Sounds disgusting," Kyle quipped.

"Ranks right up there with mushrooms," Meredith replied.

"I've had frog's legs, too."

"You're one up on me, then."

"I've even tried prairie oysters. That's deep-fried bull's testicles. A lot of fish places in the South have them on the menu."

"If you go through this gastronomical history with men you date, I'll bet you don't get kissed good-night very often."

"Some people believe that eating genitals or food suggestive of genitals makes you fertile. I learned that in a food history course."

"Higher education can be so enlightening."

"One of the girls in that class was also in my pastry class and she designed a pair of cakes shaped like . . . suggestive of . . . Anyway, everyone was impressed and told her she could make a fortune, so she dropped out of school and moved to Chicago and opened an erotic bakery."

"She'll probably make a fortune in franchises and be awarded an honorary doctorate someday."

"If she doesn't get arrested first," Meredith responded.

There was a blackboard behind the hostess's desk with the catch of the day posted on it. "Grouper," she read. "That doesn't sound very exotic."

It wasn't until they'd been escorted to a table and handed menus that Kyle's surprise was revealed.

"Alligator?" Meredith said. "Fried alligator tail?"

"Local specialty," Kyle explained. "I take it you haven't indulged before?"

"No, but I've heard it's good. It's supposed to taste like chicken, isn't it?"

"It's a little gamier, but you can handle it. Compared to prairie oysters, it's practically Grandma's Sunday pot roast."

"I never said I *liked* prairie oysters," Meredith said. "I said I'd tried them."

Fried gator tail closely resembled chicken strips in appearance, as well as taste. Meredith had just concluded that she liked the gamy flavor of the meat when Stacy began fretting. Meredith and Kyle both tried to calm her by talking to her, but failed.

"I'm going to hold her," Meredith said, undoing the straps on Stacy's seat.

"But you're eating," Kyle pointed out.

"So are all the other people in here. And they shouldn't have to listen to someone else's baby crying."

Kyle didn't argue any further. He'd noticed some censuring glares directed at their table at the height of Stacy's outburst.

Stacy grew more and more fussy, and Meredith became increasingly involved with keeping her quiet so that Kyle finished his meal before Meredith had eaten half of her gator strips.

"Here," he offered, stretching his arms out over the table. "Give her to me so you can eat."

"I don't know how much longer we can stall her," Meredith warned, carefully positioning Stacy in Kyle's strong hands. "She's not due to eat for another hour, but she's hungry."

"How can you tell?" Kyle asked, settling Stacy into his lap, bouncing her on his thigh when she showed signs of winding up to scream.

"She's sucking on her fist," Meredith explained.

Kyle looked down at Stacy and grinned. She *was* sucking on her fist. "Hey, kid," he said. "Wise up. You're not going to get anything out of there. It's not hooked up to the pump."

Between bites of gator Meredith grinned at Kyle's one-sided conversation with the baby. He'd certainly come a long way from being terrified of touching her.

A minute later Stacy screwed up her face and let out a piercing wail. Several diners turned to stare at them. One man scowled so disapprovingly that Kyle stiffened visibly. "Child prodigy," he told the man. "She's practicing for the Metropolitan Opera."

Meredith nearly choked on the alligator tail she was about to swallow and tried to control her laughter.

"The Metropolitan Opera?" she wheezed.

"You'd think the man had never heard a baby crying."

"Or doesn't like to hear one crying when he eats."

Stacy wailed again. Meredith put her napkin on the table and slid out of the booth with her arms extended. "I'm going to take her into the rest room and feed her before she caves the roof in."

Rising, Kyle handed Stacy over to her. "You didn't finish your alligator."

"Have them put it in a doggy bag for later," she said and smiled. "I, uh, noticed Key lime pie on the menu."

"I'll order us some," Kyle told her.

There was no chair in the ladies' room but there was a generous anteroom where Meredith was able to nurse Stacy standing up without being interrupted.

After her feeding, Stacy was sweet-tempered, and sat docilely in her infant seat, looking around the dining room as enthralled as a child at a circus.

"What a transformation!" Kyle said.

"Mother's magic," Meredith countered. "You know, I think the aroma of the food made her hungry. Even though she doesn't eat solid food, the smells must have stimulated her taste buds."

Kyle put his forefinger in Stacy's fist and jiggled it a bit. "Ready for some gator tail, are you? You're going to be a good Florida girl." Then, looking at Meredith, he asked, "How's the pie?"

"Not bad. But they used reconstituted lime juice."

"Picky, picky, picky," Kyle teased, extracting his finger so he could fork into his own piece.

"Wait'll you taste *my* Key lime pie," she replied. "I use fresh limes."

Back at Kyle's house, Meredith held Stacy while Kyle moved her car seat from his car back into Meredith's. While Meredith stood waiting, Champ sauntered up and rubbed against her legs, meowing. She knelt to pet him. He accepted her affection for a few seconds, then turned his attention to the paper bag that held the fried gator meat. Nose twitching, he butted the bag repeatedly, meowing loudly.

"Are you petting that mangy tomcat again?" Kyle taunted as he approached.

"I think we've found a fellow alligator connoisseur."

"Freeloader!" Kyle grumbled, watching the cat nudge the bag.

"You could pet him, you know. *He's* friendly."

Kyle knelt beside her and let his hand hover above Champ's head until the cat finally got curious enough to sniff at it. But after a quick sampling, the tomcat turned back to the bag.

Meredith laughed. "I love a cat who has his priorities straight."

Passing Stacy to Kyle, she opened the bag and took one of the gator strips out of the foil and broke it into pieces in Champ's bowl.

"Chow hound," Kyle accused when the cat attacked the meat.

"Chow cat," Meredith corrected as she followed him inside the house.

"Want to watch the other movie you rented?" Kyle asked.

"Sure," Meredith said, putting the doggy bag in the refrigerator. "Just let me wash my hands. They're covered with gator grease."

Kyle carried Stacy into the living room and sat down on the sofa. The baby made a quirky smacking sound, and Kyle looked down at her and smiled. She responded with a toothless smile that lit up her entire face, accompanied by a rumble of laughter.

"She laughed aloud," he reported when Meredith entered the room.

"She started that yesterday," Meredith replied.

"Some of the expressions on her face—do you ever wonder if she's thinking?"

"Not if, *what*," Meredith told him. "Babies think. They just can't put everything into perspective. Researchers say they get extremely frustrated before they learn to talk because no one understands them."

"What's that?" Kyle leaned his ear toward Stacy's face. "Yes, I'll tell her." Turning to Meredith, he said, "She said to tell you she would have enjoyed a taste of alligator tail."

"Tell her I'll be happy to oblige her in a couple of hours. Indirectly, of course. Right now, I'm going to watch a movie."

Kyle watched her take the film from the plastic case and slip it into the VCR. The feminine clothes she was wearing emphasized the grace of her movements, the softness of her curves. As she bent over to insert the video, his eyes were drawn to the swell of her hips under the soft pleats of the skirt, and he recalled how she'd felt in his arms, nestled against him.

You've been alone too long, he thought. *Don't forget why.*

"Do you want me to take her?" Meredith offered, settling onto the sofa.

"She seems to be comfortable where she is."

Too comfortable, Meredith reflected. It was not jealousy that unsettled her, but fear. Stacy was becoming too accustomed to Kyle. *The dilemma again.*

By the end of the movie, Stacy was sound asleep. Kyle carried her into Meredith's quarters and put her in the crib. "Will she sleep until morning?"

"That depends on how you define morning," Meredith answered. She walked with Kyle into the kitchen. There was a distinct flavor of a date ending, along with all the attendant awkwardness.

They said each other's names at the same time, then laughed self-consciously.

"Thank you for dinner," Meredith said.

"I enjoyed the company."

"And thank you for introducing me to alligator tail."

"My pleasure."

Meredith gave a soft laugh. "I can't believe you told that man Stacy was a child prodigy practicing for the Metropolitan Opera."

"He was a boor."

"Well, you straightened him out."

They fell silent for a moment. Then Kyle asked, "Are you wearing perfume?"

"No," Meredith replied, surprised by the question.

"I thought . . . just since we got back to the house—"

"Oh!" Meredith exclaimed, comprehension dawning. "It must be the hand lotion I bought today. I put some on after I washed my hands."

Kyle reached for her hand, guided it to his face and sniffed. "It's nice."

"It was on sale."

"You should wear it more often." He squeezed her hand firmly. "Then again," he told her, lowering his face to hers, "maybe you shouldn't."

She closed her eyes as his lips brushed hers tentatively. Then she took a deep breath and reopened her eyes. "That's dangerous," she warned. "I'm the woman who eats frog's legs and prairie oysters, remember?"

"All I tasted were Key lime pie and woman," he said, pulling her into his embrace.

Meredith slid her hands over his shoulders. She tilted her head in invitation. His face dipped to meet hers.

The kiss was slow, unhurried; there was no urgency as their mouths hovered an inch apart for what seemed an eternity of seconds before their lips met tentatively, then melded in mutual acceptance of the pleasure they were sharing. They parted with the same slowness before their kiss lost its sweetness and innocence.

For a moment, they remained close while Meredith laid her cheek against Kyle's shoulder. She listened to the sound of his heart beating while he relished the silky-soft texture of her hair under his chin. Her hands fell away from his neck as she lifted her head and gave him a shy smile. His hands moved to rest lightly on her waist before relinquishing contact with her.

"Good night," they both spoke at once, then laughed nervously at their timing.

Finally Meredith sighed, then said "Good night" again, with a note of finality.

Kyle nodded without speaking and watched her disappear into her quarters.

10

MEREDITH DID NOT sleep well that night. It had been such a nice day, a pleasant evening; it had seemed natural that Kyle should kiss her, that she should let him, that she should enjoy being kissed. But in the silent darkness of her quarters, as she lay between clean sheets on a mattress still firm with newness, what had seemed so natural then, now seemed inappropriate and foolhardy.

In the wake of a new haircut, an evening of leisure and the company of an attractive, attentive man, she had forgotten the chasm of economics and social circumstances that separated her from Kyle Sawyer Brooks. He was her employer, her benefactor; she was the indigent he'd taken in and given shelter. How could she have forgotten that, even for one moment?

He had kissed her. She had let him. She had kissed him back. Kissed him back—knowing that he'd been pressured into taking her in, and that he resented her impingement on his life. She had kissed him back, knowing that he blamed her for having placed faith in the wrong person, that he believed she was a victim because she allowed herself to be victimized.

But he'd blotted her tears and understood why she was crying. He'd cradled her child in his arms. He'd complimented her when she desperately needed to be complimented, talked to her when she needed to talk. He'd held her when she needed to be held.

She lay awake staring at the bars of light that slid through the blinds he'd installed and listed all the reasons she should not have kissed him, while her body remembered the rightness of his kiss and the comfort of his embrace. She reminded herself that she was his client—his *pro bono* case—as well as his domestic employee; and either ruled out a personal relationship between them. She reminded herself that her circumstances precluded getting involved with any man until she was self-sufficient. But while she reminded herself of all the reasons why she shouldn't be involved with Kyle Sawyer Brooks, she also recalled the gentleness of his kiss and the contentment she'd experienced in the circle of his arms.

They were living together. Not "together," but in the same house. She'd been so preoccupied with the need for a roof over her head and a secure home for Stacy that she hadn't even considered the moral ramifications of their living arrangements. At first, Kyle had seemed so brusque, so aloof, so...superior and...old, that it hadn't occurred to her that she might become attracted to him. And the possibility of him becoming interested in her *in that way* had seemed so remote as to be laughable.

But he'd kissed her, and she'd kissed him back; and now their living together was a problem. Another problem. A new problem.

Meredith rolled over, squeezed her eyes shut and groaned. She'd known her respite in his house was temporary, that she would have to leave. She'd just wanted—needed—so badly to have a period of security and comfort while she built up her strength and self-esteem. It had been there for her—security, a job, a chance to piece her broken life back together, the promise of recovery and redemption. The answer to desperate prayers.

Until they'd kissed.

KYLE LUMBERED along the hallway, his feeling of dread growing with every step. His suit was perfectly pressed, his shirt wrinkle-free and a silk tie hung around his neck, its end flopping over his chest waiting to be tied into a perfect Windsor.

He was strongly tempted to duck out the front door instead of going into the kitchen. The scent of baking muffins indicated that Meredith was preparing breakfast. But his briefcase was still on the desk off the kitchen, and he needed the paperwork inside it. Even if he didn't have that reason for going through the kitchen instead of out through the front door, he wouldn't deliberately hurt Meredith by blatantly avoiding her. Besides, no problem was ever solved by avoidance. He could duck out the front door now, but eventually he'd have to come back to the house. Eventually they'd run into each other.

She was working at the counter with her back to the door. Kyle stopped just inside the kitchen, nervously waiting for the moment when she would turn around. Finally she did, carrying flatware to set the table.

He spoke her name. Slowly, hesitantly, she raised her head to meet his gaze. He read in her eyes the same confusion and ambivalence he was feeling. The questions. The embarrassment. The guilt. The regret.

"It shouldn't have happened," she said softly.

Kyle felt like laughing aloud with relief. He hadn't been certain how she'd interpret—or misinterpret—his kissing her. As bad as this awkward moment *was*, it would have been far *worse* if he'd found her humming some cheerful little ditty and glorying in the role of homemaker.

"It was—"

"A mistake," Meredith finished flatly.

The tinge of pain in her voice hurt him. "No. It wasn't a mistake, it was just . . . the moment. It was human reaction."

She closed her eyes and sighed, then focused her attention on setting the table. "We can't *react* that way again."

"We won't."

Her gaze met his—that gray gaze he found so disconcerting.

"We're adults," he said, feeling somehow as though he were losing an argument.

"That's the problem."

"It was just the moment," he repeated. "Now that we know what can . . ." He hesitated. "We'll be on guard."

Holding the back of a chair in a white-knuckled grip, she nodded without looking at him.

After a pause, Kyle covered her hand with his and used his free hand to guide her chin up so that his eyes compelled her attention. "I kissed you because I enjoyed your company. I didn't do it to cheapen you."

Several seconds ticked by before she replied, "I'm just trying to survive."

"I know," he said, tension knotting his gut as he fought back an urge to brush his thumb over the smoothness of her cheek. They remained frozen, each captivated by the other, until the oven timer shrilled and Meredith spun around to take the muffins from the oven with apparent relief.

Kyle poured himself a cup of coffee, sat down at the table and watched her put the muffins in a basket, trying not to notice her graceful movements—of which he was now acutely conscious. It didn't matter that she was back in her usual jeans and T-shirt; he had seen her in a dress and was aware of her innate femininity. His mind and heart perversely refused to forget that inside her sneakers, her toenails were painted hot pink. Because, she'd said, the polish was on sale and she'd been delighted to be able to reach her toes again after being pregnant.

He had held her and now noted the female narrowness of her shoulders, the nip of her waist, the swell of her hips. He had kissed her, and now he found it impossible to set aside the tactile memory of her lips, full and pliant, under his as he looked at her face when she set the basket of muffins on the table in front of him.

He busied himself buttering a muffin, pouring milk over cereal and drinking his coffee. Although she had set two places, she did not join him, but disappeared into her quarters. He heard her talking to Stacy, and found the timbre of her voice soothing even though he couldn't distinguish the words. Again he felt grudging respect for her—for her tenacity, for her devotion to her daughter, for her determination and quickness of mind. Meredith had immediately comprehended the danger of that kiss, and its threat to the tenuous status quo of their relationship. Another woman might have tried to exploit the attraction that had developed between them.

He was relieved that she didn't return while he ate his breakfast; even more relieved when she called out a goodbye after he called to her before leaving the house.

Meredith listened for the sound of his car's engine before she went back into the kitchen to eat breakfast. The inevitable confrontation hadn't been as awful as she'd feared; he hadn't agreed with her that the kiss had been a mistake, but he had agreed that it had been an error in judgment.

Just the moment. Human reaction.

It had felt like more to her. Even though she recognized it as a mistake, it had felt timeless and personal.

I kissed you because I enjoyed your company.

Maybe it had been more personal to him than he cared to admit.

I didn't do it to cheapen you.

Meredith knew he was sincere. The integrity of the kiss somehow made it more formidable. If it had been just another grab, she might be able to get angry enough at Kyle to forget that she liked him. But liking him made it . . . Even as they'd discussed the folly of what had happened, she'd been unable to ignore the sheer maleness of him, the open shirt collar that eventually would be buttoned when he knotted the tie hanging so intimately untied over his chest.

She had lost her innocence to Thomas Castor, and now she perceived Kyle Sawyer Brooks with a woman's knowledge rather than as a girl's fantasy. When once a kiss would have set her dreaming about love and forever-after, now it made her cautious.

Her attraction to Kyle made her vulnerable, but she refused to be weak, as well. Being tempted did not mean she had to succumb to the attraction.

That decided, she launched into her daily housekeeping routine—freshening the bathrooms and sorting laundry during Stacy's morning nap, dashing to the supermarket between Stacy's midday feeding and her afternoon nap. After preparing chili to simmer until Kyle came home, she put the last coat of paint on her chest of drawers. As soon as the chest was ready to come inside, she'd be able to organize the underwear and miscellany stored in a suitcase on the floor of her closet.

How ironic, she thought, that she should finish furnishing the maid's quarters now, when the temporariness of her stay in the house had just become so evident. She was already able to wear most of her clothes. In a couple of weeks she'd find a baby-sitter for her days off and start hunting for a job with potential. Perhaps Father Mark would be able to refer her to someone reliable.

With so many restaurants in so many hotels, she should be able to find a post as sous chef to some temperamental culinary genius who would appreciate an assistant who didn't mind working hard and showed a willingness to learn. Eventually, she should get a shot as chef.

Of course, even if she found a job elsewhere, she would be dependent on her position as Kyle's housekeeper until she could save enough money for another place to live. If Kyle should manage to get some financial settlement out of Thomas, that would help. And child support would help with quality day-care and, eventually, a good preschool for Stacy.

She was not without hope or potential; still she was overcome by a bout of impatience, realizing that nothing could be done immediately. All she could do for now was perform well as Kyle's housekeeper and wait to execute her plans at the right time.

Kyle was late returning from work, and she wondered if he were purposely staying away to avoid another awkward encounter like the scene at breakfast. But he came in at half past seven, looking worn and glad to be home.

"Bad day?" Meredith asked as he sat down to a bowl of the steaming chili.

"A killer. One of those Murphy's Law days, where everything that can go wrong, does."

Meredith had eaten earlier, but she sat down at the table to keep Kyle company. She was holding Stacy. "So, what went wrong?"

"Mitzi, my receptionist, called in for personal leave because her kid had some bug, so everything was chaotic all day. Then one of my clients came down with a virus in the middle of our consultation."

"What kind of virus?"

"Something that's going around. Stomach, fever, aches and pain. I think it's the same bug Mitzi's son had."

"And your client came down with it in your office?"

"Apparently it's quite sudden. She was fine one minute, then she paled and got kind of green around the gills, if you know what I mean. By the time I asked her if she was okay she was tossing her cookies in the wastebasket."

"Yuck!"

"I finally got her down on the sofa with a wet towel on her head and called her family. She was moaning and groaning by the time they half carried her out."

"Are you sure that's all it was? A virus?"

"Yeah. According to Mitzi, it's one of those things that comes on suddenly, makes you feel like you're dying, then goes away as quickly as it comes."

"You say it's going around?"

"Apparently. Mitzi's son got it at school, and my client managed to rasp out that it had been going around at her office. If she hadn't, I'd probably have called an ambulance instead of her mother."

Meredith looked down at her daughter. "I hope Stacy doesn't get it. That kind of thing can be dangerous in babies. They get dehydrated so easily."

"Well, if she shows any signs, we'll get her to an emergency room." He grabbed Stacy's foot and tugged at it teasingly. "You're not going to make us do that, are you?"

She answered with a broad, toothless smile. "I didn't think so," Kyle said.

"She's getting a certain amount of immunity through my milk while she's nursing," Meredith explained. "Let's just hope the vitamins they sent home from the hospital with me have built up my resistance. I'm not usually susceptible to bugs, anyway."

"Neither am I," Kyle replied. "The only time I ever caught one was back when I was in college. Everyone in the dorms had been burning the midnight oil studying for midterms, and we all got it. It was like a battle zone."

For the next three days, Kyle was annoyed by the effects of the virus on his caseload. He had one case postponed because a judge got the virus. Another was disrupted when a bailiff became ill in the middle of some pertinent testimony. Mitzi caught the bug from her son and he had to call in a temp to restore some order to his office. But his quest for order was again stymied when his office manager came down with the virus and had to go home, leaving the temp without supervision. In exasperation, he finally closed down the office and hired an answering service to handle his calls.

"You're home early," Meredith commented.

"I surrendered to fate," Kyle said, detailing the crisis situation.

"Things should be back to normal by Monday," Meredith encouraged.

"They couldn't get any worse," Kyle said. "Is there anything to eat around here? I was too busy trying to keep the office from falling apart to get lunch."

"There's some leftover roast beef. How about a sandwich?"

"Great! I'm ravenous."

"Hot, au jus, or cold?"

"Cold's okay. A little mustard and some sliced onion if we've got one."

He sat down at the place she'd set for him. "Stacy napping?" he asked, picking up his sandwich.

"She fell asleep about half an hour ago," Meredith replied, dropping into a chair across from Kyle's. "She's taking longer and longer to drift off in the afternoon lately."

"Good sandwich," Kyle commented after downing a generous bite. He'd eaten over half of it before he put what was left on his plate and stared down intensely. He paled.

"Kyle?"

"I don't—" Tilting his head back, he looked around the room frantically.

"My bathroom!" Meredith told him, extending her arm in the direction of her quarters.

Kyle made a mad dash through her room into the small bathroom. After checking that he hadn't collapsed on the way, Meredith went into the kitchen to prepare a small glass of warm salt water. She took it to him. "Rinse and gargle."

Still shaky, he did as instructed. When he'd put the glass on the counter with a clumsy thunk, Meredith raised his arm and poked her head under his arm, stretching her own arm across his back to support him. "Come on. We've got to get you into bed."

She took him to his bedroom and folded back the covers on his bed. "Can you make it from here?"

He nodded, trembling with weakness. She raised her hand to his cheek. It was clammy and cool. "No fever yet."

"I'm just a little—"

"Obviously," she said. "Look, you get undressed and get into bed. I'll check on you later."

"You don't have to—"

She gave him a no-nonsense look. "Call me if you need anything."

Later on, he developed a fever, and she blotted his brow, cheeks and neck with a damp washcloth. Kyle grasped her wrist. "Thank you."

He looked weak, and was shivering and perspiring at the same time. His sudden vulnerability was a stark contrast to his usual cocky self-assurance.

"Can I get you anything?" she asked. He shook his head. "I'll be back later." He nodded.

Within an hour he was asleep. Two hours later he was awake and miserable, and she brought him lemon-flavored thirst quencher over crushed ice. "Drink it slowly," she advised. "See how it sets on your stomach."

He drank a few sips, then forced a smile through fever-parched lips. "You're a good nurse."

"I've had enough experience at it." She picked up the washcloth and carried it into his bathroom to rinse it with fresh water, then perched on the edge of the bed to blot his face again. Her hip brushed his ribs, and her body warmed from the unnatural warmth of his. *He* was ill; she was quite healthy, with healthy human responses. "How's the stomach?"

"Like an active volcano."

"You'd better not try to drink anymore right now, then."

She continued nursing him, bringing him the thirst quencher so he wouldn't get dehydrated, mopping his brow when fever made him restless and miserable.

On Saturday afternoon she found him groaning and restlessly moving around in the bed.

"What hurts?"

"Every muscle in my body."

"Roll over on your stomach," she said. "I'll give you a massage."

She found petroleum jelly in the bathroom, lubricated her hands and kneaded his aching flesh, starting with his shoulders.

"This is beyond the call of duty," he purred.

"Simple human compassion," she explained.

"Where did you learn to do this?" He sighed as she swept her hands over his back in quick, long strokes.

"I took care of my mother. Toward the end, there wasn't much I could do except try to make her comfortable." She couldn't help thinking then of her mother—of her mother's shrunken, diseased body—and contrasting it in her mind with this healthy one. Kyle was ill, but only temporarily. And his body was firm and fit—and male.

She considered lowering the sheet and massaging his legs, but turned her attention to his hands instead. Kyle sighed contentedly as she rubbed her thumbs in a circular motion up his arms, first the left, then the right.

"Feel any better?" she asked.

"Remind me to give you a raise," he murmured into his pillow. It was almost worth a case of flu to have her touching him again. "What time is it?"

"About five o'clock."

"I've had this . . . virus over twenty-four hours?"

"You'll be as good as new by morning. I'll bring you toast and hot tea for breakfast."

He groaned. "If I live that long."

She smiled, amused by his typical male response to illness. "The prognosis for survival and complete recovery is good," she assured him.

She massaged his back again before leaving, trying to maintain a clinical detachment as she ministered the basic nursing care. She tried not to notice the masculine beauty of his body, the firmness of his muscles under her fingertips.

As promised, she brought him toast and hot tea for breakfast on Sunday morning. "How do you feel?"

"Totally recovered and ravenous."

"Take it slow," she warned. "Don't overexert yourself, or you could relapse."

"How did you know strawberry preserves are my favorite?"

"There was a two-pound jar in the refrigerator. I made a wild guess."

He caught her hand and said her name tentatively.

She looked at him expectantly.

"Thanks for . . ." He sighed softly and let go of her hand. "Thanks."

She shrugged. "I didn't do that much."

Their gazes locked in silent communication. "You were here," he said softly. "You . . . took care of me."

"You were ill."

A silence followed. Finally Meredith spoke: "I'll be back for your tray."

Kyle fought back the urge to ask her to stay with him while he ate, then felt abandoned when she left. He ate his meal and waited. And waited. Although the clock told him only ten minutes had passed, it seemed longer. Finally, too restless after his confinement to stay still anymore, he decided it was time to leave his bed, get cleaned up and rejoin the world.

Meredith checked on Stacy before returning to Kyle's room for the breakfast tray. Stacy was sleeping contentedly in the crib with her little bottom in the air. Smiling, Meredith stood next to the crib for a few moments before leaning over to press a gentle kiss on her daughter's temple. *Sleep in peace, little one.*

In Kyle's room, she found the bed tray on the floor and the bed empty. The sound of running water in the bathroom solved the mystery of the missing patient. *So he was up and about, taking a shower. That was a positive sign.*

Her gaze fell on the disheveled bed. A sickbed. *But not for long,* she thought, bending over to strip away the bedding. She wadded it into a ball, which she tossed into the hallway on her way to the linen closet for fresh sheets.

In contrast to the floral percales that had been on the guest-room bed, Kyle had two sets of sheets for the king-size bed in his own room: one navy blue, which she'd just removed, the other a geometric print. She carried the print set to the bed and began spreading, smoothing and tucking. She'd just tossed the bedspread over the foot of the bed and was pulling it straight when the door to the bathroom opened.

Kyle walked out wearing a towel.

Caught off guard, still holding the edge of the bedspread in her hand, Meredith regarded him, embarrassed at first, then fascinated by the sight of him freshly scrubbed and on the verge of nudity.

"Meredith," he said.

Her face colored and she quickly averted her gaze. "I was . . . I thought you'd like fresh bedding after sweating off that fever."

Although she turned her back to him then, furiously straightening the bedspread, she sensed his presence as he walked toward her, anticipated his touch before his hand capped her shoulder. She froze, then sighed. Her shoulder sagged under the weight of his hand. All the resolve, all the logical arguments against the feelings his touch stirred in her, melted away.

She turned, knowing he was going to kiss her, knowing she wanted him to, knowing that the last thing in the world she needed was to fall in love with the man to whom she was so indebted; knowing that she *had* in fact, fallen in love with him. She could almost believe he loved her, too, as he whispered her name like the tenderest of endearments and cradled her face in his hands. That simple, whispered word crept over her senses with aphrodisiac effect. Sexual yearning spread through her entire body, warming her fingers, her toes, her ears.

"You were here for me," he said. "You took care of me."

"You needed me."

"I still need you." No hesitation. No hyperbole.

She tried to look away, turn her head, as though by not looking into his eyes she wouldn't hear his persuasive words. But his hands still cradled her face, holding it captive, just as his eyes forced her to look at him.

"I need you desperately," he murmured. "More desperately than I would have believed or you could ever understand." He kissed her then, gently at first and then more intensely, as he wrapped his arms around her.

The kiss deepened; it expanded; it became the boundaries of the universe in which they existed. And Meredith acknowledged her love for him. Despite his flaws, his foibles and what she had interpreted as his arrogance, she loved him. Never again would she see any man as the idealized manifestation of a romantic fantasy. She saw Kyle Sawyer Brooks exactly as he was and loved him anyway; loved the good things in him despite his flaws, loved him, while recognizing the differences between them.

His tongue brushed teasingly over her lips and she opened her mouth, opened herself to the kiss, to the pleasure and the passion and the risk of loving him. He held her tightly, anchoring her body close while the kiss became intense.

Meredith was slow to realize that the towel had fallen and only the soft, worn denim of her jeans separated them as his hands splayed over her buttocks to pull her body hard against his.

Breaking away from the kiss, she opened her eyes and saw in the depths of his eyes that powerful need, and believed that, at least for the moment, he really did need her.

"Don't leave me now," he pleaded.

She made a move to draw away, but his embrace was firm; the need in his eyes, mesmerizing. He slid his arms upward to cross them over her back and guided her cheek to his chest. She listened to the sound of his heart as he rested his just-shaved chin on her temple.

"I need you as much now as I did when I was sick."

The towel lay on the floor in a heap, leaving him exposed. His eyes and his voice exposed him, too; exposed the need rooted inside him. It was to that need she responded—not simply to the imposing perfection of his body, and not simply to the human weakness of desire.

He recognized the acquiescence in her silence, in the gentle touch of her hands on his ribs. "I'll protect you," he said. "You know what I mean."

Her cheek rubbed against his chest as she nodded. She'd seen the condoms in the medicine cabinet while tidying up.

He kissed the top of her head before striding to the bathroom. She watched with fascination the lithe movements of his body as he walked, the interplay of sleek muscles in his thighs and buttocks.

He returned quickly, and found her standing exactly where she'd been when he left. He could tell by the tension in her body as he took her into his arms again that she was reconsidering her decision to stay. Instead of using words to reassure her, he opted for a kiss.

Gentle, silent, poignant, the kiss set the tone for their lovemaking. Without ending the kiss, he guided her to the bed, and they sank onto the crisp, fresh sheets in a tangle of arms and legs. Still kissing her, he slid his hands beneath her T-shirt and pushed it up, caressing her flesh as he bared it, until his fingers encountered her bra. He tore his mouth from the sweetness of hers to look at her while he searched for the clasp of her bra.

Meredith touched the sides of his face with her fingertips to get his attention. Her eyes held an apology as she said, "That probably needs to stay on."

Comprehension dawned visibly on his face and he smiled tenderly, then dropped a row of hummingbird kisses along the edges of the cotton bra cups while his hand rested on her midriff. He laid his cheek on her sternum and listened to the steady beat of her heart.

You give so much—so very, very much. He longed for the right words to express the thought aloud, but words of admiration did not come as easily to him as courtroom arguments. Perhaps she understood what he wanted to tell her, though, as she combed her fingers caressingly into his hair and sighed.

When he moved, it was to kiss the smooth skin over her ribs and then lower, down to the waistband of her jeans. He was better with snaps and zippers than with words, and thanks to her cooperation, soon tossed her jeans aside.

He admired her well-shaped legs, and slid his hand over the top of her right thigh and higher, until it rested on the jut of her pelvic bone. Spying the stretch marks, still pink and well-defined, above her bikini panties, he traced one with his forefinger.

Meredith closed her eyes and sighed. "Battle scars," she explained.

Kyle kissed one of the lines from end to end, then moved up to plunder her mouth in a searing kiss, telling her without words that he found her beautiful and desirable. She wrapped her arms around him, spreading her hands over the muscles of his back, and rolled toward his heavier weight on the mattress. She crooked her leg over his, hooking her calf behind his knee, bringing their bodies into intimate alignment.

Every touch, each caress, all their discoveries and explorations carried them away from awareness of anything beyond each other and the human need driving them toward physical fulfillment. Eventually her panties were discarded and the condom was in place.

He watched her face as their bodies joined, saw a slight wince. But before he could ask about it, Meredith guided his mouth to hers and locked her legs around his and they kissed deeply while their entwined bodies searched frenetically for the complementary rhythms that would release them from their delicious torment of desire.

Meredith clung to Kyle, grasping his shoulder muscles with her hands, moving with him, against him. Kyle felt her body contracting around him as she reached her release, caressing him in the most intimate way a woman can caress a man, and he surrendered himself to the same satisfying fate.

Afterward, he held her folded in his arms and listened while her breathing returned to normal. He wanted to tell her how much her being with him meant to him, but that sounded too trite. He wanted to tell her about all the different ways he needed her in his life, but the realization of it was still too new. He wanted to tell her how he admired her generosity and selflessness. But words of endearment, so long out of use in his vocabulary, stuck through his throat.

So he simply held her while he inhaled the scent of her lotion as he brought her hand to his lips, and hoped that she would understand the tender sentiments inherent in his silence. He fell asleep with that hope strong in his heart.

When he awoke, she was no longer beside him.

11

KYLE LISTENED with fierce concentration for some sound that would tell him she was still in the house. The faint hum of the clothes washer reassured him.

He dressed quickly, pausing in the middle of brushing his teeth when he caught sight of the towel hanging on the towel bar. Meredith must have picked it up and draped it neatly over the bar on her way out of the bedroom. Kyle stared at it, grinning, picturing her stooping to pick up the towel and then carrying it into the bathroom, carefully aligning it on the bar so that it hung just so. Little Miss Fix-It.

She could fix you if you'd let her.

She'd already made him face his need for human companionship, which he'd been suppressing for such a long while.

In the kitchen, he found Stacy in her infant seat, centered on the work island. She was wide-awake, regarding the world around her with open-eyed awe. Kyle sandwiched her tiny hand between his thumb and forefinger and spoke to her. "Hi, cutie. Where's your mom?"

Stacy made a lip-smacking sound, then smiled. Kyle smiled back at her, enchanted as always by her innocent acceptance of life. "I'll bet she's not far away," he told Stacy, then whispered, "I think I hear her in the laundry room."

He walked to the door of the room. Both the washer and dryer were running, and Meredith was folding underwear and socks she'd just removed from the dryer. Pleased by the sight of her, he waited until she noticed him instead of making his presence known. He felt boyish anticipation as he imagined the expression on her face when she turned around and discovered him there.

Reality fell short of his fantasy. When her eyes met his, there was no blush of pleasure as if she recalled their lovemaking; there were no knowing, private little smiles, not even a flash of self-consciousness. He saw the converse of his own jubilant mood in her morose expression, and regret reflected in her eyes where happy memories should be.

"It shouldn't have happened," she said.

Weighed down with disappointment, Kyle took a long time to respond. Meredith went back to folding laundry, obviously as a form of escape.

"You're wrong," he answered finally.

She stopped working but didn't look at him. "Am I?"

"Don't diminish it."

Her sigh was rife with disillusionment. Her shoulder blades stood out against her shirt as she braced her arms on the edge of the folding table. "I couldn't diminish it if I wanted to. It was—" there came another sigh "—monumental." She shook her head slowly, and gave a short, mirthless laugh. "To think we were concerned about a kiss."

"This was different."

"Oh, yes." She spun around and glared at him, crossing her arms over her waist in challenge. "Human reaction on a grand scale."

"It was more than that. It was . . . a beginning."

"Of what?"

"Of—" He choked on the word *us*. Her attitude had shocked him down to his toes; he'd been unprepared for hostility.

"You can't say it," she challenged. "I don't even want to think it."

"It's not what you think," he said urgently, feeling that something precious was slipping away and not knowing how to hold on to it. "Don't turn it into something ugly."

"I don't have to do that. It's ugly enough already."

Fighting to control himself, Kyle stepped into the small room and wrapped his fingers loosely around the top of her arm. Deliberately crowding her, he moved closer and spoke with his face scarcely an inch above hers. "I wasn't using you. Look at me and tell me that you believe that."

Her expression said everything he didn't want to hear. She didn't believe him, not only in her mind, but in her heart. And since her heart was still tender from the lashing Castor had given it, he realized he was inheriting her accumulated suspicion and rage at men.

"You're wrong," he told her. "You're so far off base you're not even in the ballpark."

"I should have had enough sense to stay out of the game."

"What do you want from me? An apology?"

She glared at him.

"I'm not sorry," he said.

Stacy's cries provided her a convenient escape. She bolted past Kyle with an air of escape that somehow made him feel tainted. That she could make him feel guilty irritated him. He'd been feeling so . . . cleansed. Renewed. Pleased to discover that he still could care;

pleased, even, to discover that he still gave a damn about his ability to care.

Stacy was crying in earnest when Meredith reached her. Meredith took her out of the seat, patted her back and uttered reassurances, although at the moment she felt like the last person on earth qualified to reassure anyone about anything.

She was so filled with pessimism, she felt there was no room for hope in any form. How could she have done it? Hadn't she learned anything from her experience with Thomas?

Stupid! It was bad enough that she had fallen for a creep like Thomas Castor in the first place, but at least she hadn't known what a creep he was, up front. With Kyle—Kyle Sawyer Brooks—she had no defense—no reason beyond stupidity. She'd toppled into love with him with her eyes wide open, knowing all the reasons she shouldn't. He was her benefactor, her boss, her attorney and, in some ways, her harshest, most unyielding judge. They were diametrically opposed philosophically; a universe apart, economically.

She'd thought he was the vulnerable one in that bedroom, but it had been she who was vulnerable. Vulnerable, because despite all logic, she had fallen in love and was unable to resist the one thing capable of breaking down her defenses—his need. He had needed her; he'd said so. And because she'd fallen in love with him and understood what it was to need, she'd given in to his pleas.

It was only afterward, while he slept and she'd been left alone in the silence of that room, that she'd realized the limitations of his need for her. His was a passing need, a physical one, while hers...hers was a voracious emotional need for someone to care about her, someone to respect her, to provide unwavering support—for someone to believe in her.

Human reaction. Both their needs had been real, and human. But they were mismatched, and their needs were equally mismatched. He had reached for her because he needed physical fulfillment, and she had stepped into his arms because she needed emotional companionship.

It had been glorious—until he'd fallen asleep and she'd remained awake to ponder the folly of what she'd done. Until she'd realized what had been said—and what *hadn't*. He hadn't said he loved her—not even that she was special to him.

Thank God she hadn't poured out her heart to him! If she'd done that, they'd both know what a fool she was.

Pressing her cheek against Stacy's head, she sighed. As if he didn't know already! As if he cared. Did he care beyond convenience? He'd said he kissed her because he enjoyed being with her. But who was to say that he wouldn't have enjoyed being with anyone who happened to be there?

Enjoying a person's company was a far cry from being in love. Only fools seemed to forget the difference.

"Did I hurt you?"

She jerked around at the sound of his voice. How was she supposed to answer a question like that? Had he hurt her? He had used her, compromised her. And because she'd allowed herself to fall in love with him and granted him the power, he had broken her heart.

Had he hurt her? Her only answer was a glare filled with pain.

"I saw you wince when . . . I didn't hurt you, did I?"

Physical pain. Something tangible—that, she could handle.

"It was uncomfortable for a moment. I had some stitches. The doctor told me to anticipate a little discomfort."

"Are you all right? It wasn't dangerous, this soon after having a baby?" His concern for her was genuine.

"It's been long enough. There was...just what I said, what the doctor told me to anticipate...just a twinge of discomfort at first."

"I wouldn't purposely hurt you. You must know that."

Meredith closed her eyes and fought back a scream of frustration and rage. Sensing her mother's tension, Stacy began fussing again. "She's tired," Meredith said. "I'm going to try to rock her to sleep."

Kyle watched Meredith's door close, feeling that it had been figuratively slammed in his face. *Damn! What had he done that was so terrible?*

He sat down at the table and waited for Meredith to come out of the room. He waited. And brooded. Finally, giving up on her, he opened the refrigerator in search of food. Two pieces of toast didn't go far toward appeasing a two-day fast.

Since he'd decided Meredith was deliberately closeting herself away from him, he was surprised when the door to her quarters opened and she walked into the kitchen. "That's chicken soup in the deli carton," she said. "I thought you'd want to progress into solid food gradually."

"That's what you thought, is it?" He grabbed the deli container and thrust it against her sternum, forcing her to raise her hand to take it.

She gave him a puzzled look.

"Tell me, did you buy animal crackers to go with it, or do I have to make do with saltines?"

"You'll have to make do with saltines," Meredith replied, emptying the carton into a saucepan. "Since you never gave me a list of foods you liked, I didn't know you had a fondness for animal crackers."

"You'd have bought some, wouldn't you? If I'd made out a stupid list and said that I liked Belgian chocolate and canned smoked oysters, you'd have bought them, and had them up there in the pantry, wouldn't you?"

"Is that supposed to be some sort of accusation?"

"You're just too efficient."

"Is that a complaint?"

"Hell, yes, it's a complaint! I don't understand you at all. What was this morning supposed to be? Part of the deluxe service?"

Meredith winced momentarily, but refused to give in to the hysteria that threatened to overwhelm her. "Yes," she said, forcing herself to match his sarcastic tone. "That's what it was. You're very astute to pick up on it."

"I'm more astute than you think," he responded, deadly serious. "Astute enough to know that you're doing this about-face because it *wasn't* part of the service."

"Either way, it was a mistake."

"A blissful one."

"It was just *human reaction*."

"In its highest form, my dear."

"Don't 'my dear' me. I'm your housekeeper, not your *dear*." She impatiently drove a spoon through the heating soup.

"If looks could heat, that soup would be boiling over."

She scowled, and he cringed from her.

"For a comedian, you're a pretty good attorney."

"For a shrew, you're not such a bad person."

She glared at him again, then flung open a cabinet door to take out a bowl, which she plunked on the counter.

"I think you like me a little bit," he ventured.

She poured the soup into the bowl and carried it to the table. "Your lunch is ready."

He sat down. "Do I get a spoon, or do I drink it straight from the bowl?"

She slapped a spoon onto the table so forcefully that the bowl rattled.

"Hit a nerve, did I?" he asked.

"So what?" she snapped.

"It makes a difference if you like me, you know."

"It was still a mistake."

"What if I said I like you, too?"

"It *doesn't* make any difference!" she retorted. "Don't you see that? You're still . . . *Kyle Sawyer Brooks*, and I'm still the homeless indigent you took in."

"You seem to be having a lot more trouble forgetting that than I am." He sipped some of the steaming soup out of his spoon, burned his mouth, then emitted a less-than-refined word in reaction.

"Maybe being homeless was a bigger thing to me than being Kyle Sawyer Brooks is to you."

Kyle suddenly saw, with a shocking clarity, the situation from Meredith's perspective, and understood how the inequalities she perceived undermined what they'd shared. He realized that, as skewed as he believed her perception was—by factors that were meaningless to him, he couldn't deny that—it was *truth* to Meredith.

Money was of crucial importance to people who didn't have it. Likewise food and shelter. To him, his role as her benefactor was but a small part of a much larger agenda. To her, however, it was paramount, titanic. She could not set it aside, treat it as unimportant, even if she wanted to. She was different from his clients who became fixated on one possession—the house, the yacht, the dog—and were hell-bent on getting legal ownership of it because it symbolized all the conflict in their failed marriages. The precariousness of her situation was simply too important an element in her life to ignore. He'd been "stuck" with a housekeeper who needed a place to live, whereas she'd been destitute and desperate; and what to him had been a minor imposition thrust on him by Mark, had been to her a way of escape from that destitution and desperation.

He could argue all day that it didn't matter, but to no avail. It didn't matter to him; it mattered a great deal to her. How they'd come together was less important to him than the fact that out of all the people in the world, *they'd* come together. His career and social circle provided him more than adequate opportunities to meet women. Yet, only Meredith had managed to breach his emotional guard and touch him.

He was enough of an attorney to recognize when argument was futile. Abruptly he stood, sending his chair skittering across the floor behind him. "I'm not hungry anymore," he said, reaching into his pocket for his car keys. "Don't worry about dinner. I won't be in."

He'd planned an exit with dramatic impact, but found himself unable to stalk out without taking a backward glance—*more* than a glance.

She was tense, hugging herself, and appeared to have withered. Her eyes tore at his heart—those huge gray-colored mirrors of vulnerability and pain.

Before she could anticipate his action and stop it, he grasped her upper arms with his hands and leaned over to kiss her cheek. "We'll work on it," he promised. Then, before she could react, he made good his dramatic retreat.

Once out of the driveway, he realized he had no place to go. With no particular destination in mind, he followed the neighborhood roads to the highway and just drove. His first stop was a restaurant where he filled up the empty cavern in his stomach. His second stop, much to his own consternation, was the rectory, where he was informed that Father Mark was attending a weekend retreat in another state and would return the next night.

More frustrated than ever, he asked to use the rectory phone. "I need to call a friend of mine," he said.

A friend? he questioned, as the telephone on the other end of the line rang. *Be honest with yourself. It's an acquaintance, a peer—not a friend. You don't have any friends, no real ones. You've pushed away any that you had, except for Mark, who refused to give up. And you haven't let anyone get near you for years.*

He wangled an invitation to the business associate's house to watch the end of a ball game on television, to be followed by whatever suited their fancy at the moment. Kyle hoped that by the time he arrived, his "friend" would have taken advantage of a time-out or station break to phone a few other "friends" and they'd end up with a party of five or six, meeting at some trendy restaurant that catered to young professionals.

Kyle would be safe, surrounded by people. And no one would know he was alone in the middle of the crowd.

A few weeks earlier he wouldn't even have recognized it himself—but that was before he'd taken in a homeless woman and her hungry baby, who'd made him remember what it was like not to have to be alone.

12

FOR THE NEXT WEEK, an atmosphere of strained politeness prevailed in the house. He and Meredith were painstakingly polite and carefully distant. They spoke only when necessary.

Meredith made her message unmistakably clear by the set of her shoulders and her brisk, clipped manner: What had happened between them shouldn't have happened, and never would again.

Every time she diverted her eyes to keep from meeting his, every time she pretended to be busy in some mundane task in order to avoid acknowledging his presence, Kyle felt the sting of rejection, experiencing a pang of loss that saddened and stymied him.

Refusing to believe that there was no way to bring back the comfortable camaraderie that had led them into each other's lives and hearts, he applied logic to the problem of Meredith and reestablishing their promising relationship. Yet no approach seemed quite workable. Every possible approach he came up with struck him as either too radical or inapplicable.

The strain wore on him and, he suspected, on Meredith, too. The lethargic, automaton quality to her movements that had slowly dissipated between the time she'd gone to work for him and the time of their disastrous mistake reappeared, and she seemed edgy and tired.

On Wednesday, her afternoon off, she took the cat to the veterinarian for shots. She told him about it on Thursday morning.

"I know," he said. "The vet's secretary called my office to confirm that I would take care of the bill."

"The vet thinks we should have him fixed."

"The vet wants to make money."

"He said that if Champ could talk he would thank us for it afterward."

Kyle nearly choked on his muffin. "I seriously doubt that."

"He said that if we could spend one hour feeling what a male cat feels when a female cat is in heat and he can't get to her that there wouldn't be an unneutered tomcat left in the world."

Kyle gave Meredith a long, significant look. "You can tell the vet for me that I have a pretty good idea what sexual frustration feels like, and I'm not standing in line to be castrated just because I'm frustrated."

Meredith glared at him for a moment. "It's different with animals. To them it's pure instinct. With people it's . . . there's supposed to be more. Man is the only animal capable of reason, of thinking."

"Tell me you haven't done your share of thinking about what happened between us Sunday morning, and you'll prove once again that human beings are the only animals capable of lying, too."

"We were talking about the cat!"

"The cat. Yes. Well, you fed the cat. Now I'm preserving his dignity."

"But—"

"But nothing! A man has to draw the line somewhere, and I'm drawing it at castration!"

When he left the house a few minutes later, Champ ran to greet him. Kyle knelt and scratched the cat's chin. "I know, old buddy. I heard all about it, but don't you worry about a thing. I'm not going to let her do it to you, too."

That evening he fell into his old routine of eating dinner out in order to delay going home. Anything was easier than facing that stony, accusing silence.

Then, on Friday, he called the house and got the crisp "Brooks residence" he'd come to expect when Meredith answered the phone.

"I was hoping you'd be home," he said.

Silence. Lord, but he hated the empty sound of that silence.

"I know this is short notice, but I'd like to bring a few friends home with me tonight. Do you think you can put something together for a buffet dinner?"

"Yes." From the curtness of her reply, she might as well have added "Mr. Brooks." An awkward pause followed before she asked, "What did you have in mind?"

"Something simple. Cold cuts or something. And get everything we need to make margaritas."

"Margaritas?"

"Ask at the liquor store, they'll tell you."

"I know what goes into margaritas."

"There's some coarse salt in the cabinet in the bar, but it's been there for ages. Check it out and make sure it hasn't turned to stone. We may need to get a new box."

"All right."

"Get a couple of bottles of white wine, too. The same brand that's in the rack already. Use your judgment about anything else."

It was everything Meredith could do to keep from clicking her heels together, saluting and saying "Aye, aye, sir," before hanging up.

Well, what did you expect? You two haven't had a decent conversation in days, unless you count the discussion about having Champ fixed. Of course, he's going to treat you like the hired help. You are the hired help! You forgot it once. You can't afford to forget it again.

She made out a tentative menu, considering and discarding ideas, finally settling on finger sandwiches and vegetable and fruit trays with buttermilk- and sweet dips. She would dress up the presentation with some radish roses and turnip flowers and a yellow-squash swan or two.

With Stacy watching from her infant seat, Meredith crossed the *t* and dotted the *i* in turnip on her shopping list. "That ought to do it," she said. "We're going to wow 'em, aren't we?"

Stacy made a blubbering sound with her lips.

"Raspberries?" Meredith asked playfully, lowering her face to rub her nose against Stacy's. "We don't want raspberries." Stacy laughed, which had a sobering effect on Meredith. Under her breath she muttered, "We just don't want to embarrass the boss."

The boss. You remember the boss, Stacy. The man who owns this house. The man who talks to you and grins at you. The man Mommy fell in love with.

As if reading her mother's mind, Stacy made the blubbering sound again, and Meredith gave her a wry smile. "Yes. I know. It was a dumb thing to do. It's just . . . He's so . . ."

She sighed, then swallowed. "No excuses, kiddo. I just fell head over heels, plain and simple. It just . . . He was so nice, and I was . . . I needed someone who talks back to me when I talk. Not that I'm complaining about you, you understand. We're pals, aren't we?" Touching Stacy's foot again, she smiled a sad, bittersweet smile and was rewarded with one of Stacy's uninhibited grins.

"Yeah," Meredith said. "Pals. Well, palsy-walsy, it's time to go do some shopping. Gotta earn our keep, you know."

It was a photo finish. She had just put the last of the prepared food into the refrigerator and was grinding carrot peels in the disposal when she heard not one but two cars in the driveway. After the attendant door-slamming, there were voices and, not long afterward, the sound of the front door opening and closing.

That Kyle was using the front door caused her an unexpected twinge of disappointment, which she quickly shrugged away. Of course, he would use the front door. Had she been expecting him to come in the side door and introduce her to his guests as though she were a member of the family instead of the hired help?

In the living room, Kyle and his guests were laughing and sounding cheerful. Meredith distinguished a female voice and at least two male voices in addition to Kyle's.

She sat down at the table and propped her chin on her fist, awaiting his majesty's pleasure. Minutes later she overheard—she couldn't help eavesdropping, since the rooms were close together—Kyle tell the others that he was going to talk to his housekeeper about drinks.

"Housekeeper?" a male voice questioned. "Is that something new?"

She heard the self-conscious note in Kyle's voice. "It's a big house. I thought it was time I got some help."

"I'm green with envy," came the woman's voice—a sultry voice.

Sexy. She disliked the woman sight unseen. Disliked her for being in the living room as a guest instead of in the kitchen waiting to serve dinner. Disliked her for saying something as coy as "I'm green with envy," and for making it sound light and flirtatious.

"You got yourself a house today. Get yourself a housekeeper," Kyle said.

"Ha!" That *voice* again. "I'll be lucky to pay the electric bill after taking care of the mortgage."

Kyle laughed. "You're just going to have to find yourself a millionaire to marry, Rachel."

He ambled into the kitchen. The smile that lingered on his face faded as he nodded a self-conscious greeting to Meredith. "We're—"

"Ready for drinks," she finished, hopping up. "I couldn't help overhearing. Everything's set up at the bar. I wasn't sure whether you'd want me to mix, or if you'd want to do that yourself."

Kyle shrugged.

"Why don't I mix the first blender of margaritas, then you can take it from there," Meredith suggested.

Kyle nodded, and she preceded him into the living room. A sudden, unnatural silence filled the room as Kyle's guests halted their conversation to stare at her.

"*This* is your housekeeper?" one of the men said. He was about Kyle's age, well dressed, and he emanated an aura of joi de vivre that told even a stranger that what he was saying shouldn't be taken too seriously.

"You're just full of surprises, aren't you, Kyle!" the woman said. Meredith had been expecting a tall, statuesque blonde; Rachel was a voluptuous brunette with short, black hair and spiky bangs.

Kyle ignored the innuendo in her teasing gibe. "Everyone, this is Meredith. Meredith, meet Rachel, George and Sam."

Each of his guests nodded in turn. The jovial man was George. Sam was older, dignified and quite serious.

"Rachel just won total custody of her house," Kyle explained. "We're celebrating."

"Celebrating, hell!" Rachel exclaimed. "I'm tying one on while that creepoid ex-husband of mine removes his slimy possessions from my house under the watchful eye of an armed off-duty policeman."

"Congratulations, or whatever the proper sentiment is," Meredith responded.

"Congratulations is as good as any. But most of the credit goes to Kyle. He's the one who pulled it off."

"George is the one who uncovered the bonds your husband was hiding," Kyle reminded her.

"Ex-husband," Rachel corrected.

"Soon-to-be-ex husband," Kyle amended. To Meredith, he said, "George is a private investigator."

Meredith's face registered surprise. That affable man an investigator?

Kyle laughed at her reaction. "Looks innocuous and benign, doesn't he? That's part of what makes him so good."

George got up and strode to the bar. "Just a small part," he said, giving Meredith a thorough once-over. "I'm very, very good."

"Just ignore him," Kyle told her. "He says that to all the women."

"Only the beautiful ones," George pointed out. "Life's too short to mess with less than the best."

Kyle's mouth hardened into a line momentarily before he asked, "What are you drinking tonight, George?"

"The usual. With a twist."

"Ginger ale with a twist, it is," Kyle said, filling a highball glass with ice.

"I never drink," George announced, continuing to eye Meredith lecherously. "It dulls the wits—and the senses."

Kyle popped the top on a can of ginger ale and poured it over the ice. "You can dress him up, but you can't make him behave," he told Meredith in a stage aside. He slid the glass across the smooth surface of the bar. "Knock it off, George. She's not used to you yet."

"Why, Kyle, you sound almost jealous," Rachel commented. She sidled up next to George. "I hope that's margaritas you're mixing in that blender."

Meredith gave her a saccharin smile. "That's what Mr. Brooks ordered."

"Mr. Brooks," Rachel repeated. "Ooh, I'm impressed. I've never heard anyone call you Mr. Brooks except Creepoid's attorney."

"Meredith was just being coy, weren't you Meredith?"

"Yes, Kyle," Meredith replied.

George whistled under his breath. "Now that's compliance, Kyle. What do you use for discipline, a cattle prod or a cat-o-nine?"

"He keeps a blackboard in the kitchen and runs his fingernails over it when I get out of line," Meredith said, defusing the warning glare Kyle directed at George.

George laughed aloud. "She's sharp, Kyle. Very sharp."

"I just hope she makes a good margarita," Rachel put in. "Don't you think we could use a tiny bit more tequila?"

Skeptically raising her eyebrows, Meredith splashed another ounce of tequila into the blender.

"She's standing right here," Kyle pointed out. "Don't talk about her as though she's a piece of furniture."

George looked shocked for a moment, but quickly recovered. "I'd take furniture with her lines anytime."

Rachel shrugged contritely. "Hey, Sam, what'll it be?"

"I'll have my white wine now so it'll have time to wear off," Sam answered, joining them at the bar. "I'm the designated driver, remember?"

"You're a gem," Rachel said, wrapping her arm around his.

The blender spun into operation with a whir that prevented conversation. Seconds later, Meredith poured a generous portion of margarita into a prepared goblet, skewered a slice of lime over the salted rim and handed it to Rachel. "One margarita, heavy on the tequila."

She turned to Kyle, who was working a corkscrew into a bottle of white wine. "There's more in the blender. I'm going to start getting the buffet ready."

Once in the kitchen, she braced her arms on the counter and took a deep breath to steady herself. *What did you expect when he brought in guests? You* are *the hired help, you know.*

So, act like it! she told herself with a sigh and, peeling herself away from the counter, she went to the refrigerator for the food she'd prepared.

She arranged the food on platters and was surveying her handiwork, moving a finger sandwich here, a deviled egg there to perfect the presentation when Kyle came into the kitchen. "It's ready to serve," she told him.

"You did all this on short notice?" he asked.

"It's simple food, really. The garnishes make it look fancy."

"About what happened at the bar—"

"I didn't notice anything," she said blithely, in a way that informed him she definitely *had* noticed.

"The bit about the blackboard was classic. George was right. You're very smart."

"You learn to think on your feet when you wait tables."

Kyle frowned at her flippant tone. "We'll talk more later."

"Yes, Mr. Brooks."

He gave her a stern look before exiting.

After the hors d'oeuvres, Meredith cleared the table and brought out a tray of fruits and cold chocolate fondue. While she was passing out dessert plates, an angry yell sounded from her quarters.

"Is that a baby?" Rachel asked incredulously.

"She's been asleep for hours," Meredith replied to Kyle's lift of eyebrows.

"Go on," Kyle said. "We can handle it from here."

To Meredith's surprise, Rachel followed her out of the dining room. Meredith paused in the kitchen to ask, "Is there something I can get for you?" Surely she heard Stacy crying.

"Could I see your baby?" Rachel requested, with an odd note of desperation in her voice.

"Sure," Meredith answered, leading Rachel into her quarters. "But I have to warn you, she's been asleep since two o'clock, so she's probably going to keep on hollering her head off until she's fed."

"I'd be happy to feed her for you."

"That would be a little difficult," Meredith said, lifting Stacy from the crib.

"You're nursing!" Rachel exclaimed, as Meredith balanced her screaming daughter on her lap with one arm and worked the buttons on her blouse with her free hand. ˒acy's cries subsided abruptly as Meredith lifted her to her breast, only to be replaced by loud and enthusiastic sucking noises.

Rachel perched on the edge of Meredith's bed. Her entire face softened with yearning as she watched Stacy nurse. "I wanted children, but my husband—*ex*-husband—wanted to wait until we could afford them. Then, when we could . . . Well, Creepoid wasn't as excited about the idea of children as I was."

She sighed. "Considering the way things worked out, I guess it was just as well we didn't have any."

"Stacy's father wasn't too wild about parenthood, either. Kyle's helping me sue for child support."

"If Kyle goes after him, the money's as good as in your bank account."

"You're missing dessert," Meredith said.

"I can afford to skip dessert once in a while," Rachel replied. "I'm not making you nervous or anything? I wouldn't want to curdle your milk."

Smiling, Meredith assured Rachel that her milk wasn't easily "curdled."

"Those trays were pretty fancy," Rachel commented. "Did you do all the work yourself?"

Meredith nodded.

"Even those swans and the flowers? Where does a person learn to do stuff like that?"

"You pick it up. We had a guest chef in one of my food-preparation classes, and I worked in a couple of delis."

"Beats the hell out of actuarial tables," Rachel observed, then cut off the inevitable question with, "Don't ask. It's too boring to explain, but it has to do with insurance."

She frowned. "I supported that clown all the way through graduate school and then worked my tush off so he could get started in business and then, when he finally makes it big, whammo! He falls in love with a design engineer. I guess she looked better in a hard hat than I did in a nightie. And it didn't hurt that she was ten years younger than me."

"Men!" Meredith snorted.

"You said it," Rachel agreed. "I tell you, I don't know what I would have done without Kyle's help. He's been unbelievable. There were times when I was ready to just walk away, but Kyle wouldn't let me. He said that I could only be victimized if I allowed myself to be."

"I think I've heard that speech," Meredith remarked.

"Yeah. It's one of Kyle's favorites."

So it isn't just me. Not just because I was homeless, not just because I was a pro bono case. Kyle tells other clients the same thing about allowing themselves to be victimized.

Stacy finished nursing and Meredith changed her diaper and put her in a fresh gown, then placed her in Rachel's arms.

"She's exquisite," Rachel marveled, tracing Stacy's cheek with her fingertip. Rested from her nap and well fed, Stacy was in a good mood. She smiled.

"I've got to go show Sam," Rachel said. "He can't figure out what people see in babies. That's a banker for you. I'm trying to educate him. You don't mind, do you?"

"Not in the least," Meredith replied. "I love it when people gush over her. Just bring her back when you get tired of holding her."

"Never," Rachel said, then called out, "Sam! Sam, you've got to see this baby."

Meredith cleared the dessert plates from the table and carried them into the kitchen. A while later she heard Stacy crying, and dashed to the living room to rescue Rachel. But Kyle already had. He was bouncing Stacy on his shoulder, patting her on the back.

"I don't believe it," George commented. "You do that like an old pro."

"I *am* an old pro with this little girl. Watch, she'll smile for me." He cradled Stacy in his hands so she could see his face. "Won't you?" he said, smiling down at her.

Stacy complied, and he gave everyone an I-told-you-so nod of the head.

He's showing off! Meredith realized with a start, as she watched him coax Stacy into a belly laugh. *He's showing her off, just like a proud—*

Don't think it! she cautioned herself. *Of course, he's attached to her. Who could resist her? She's so tiny and perfect and innocent. That doesn't mean he's ready to sign up for a permanent hitch as father.*

"You're just full of surprises tonight, Kyle," Rachel observed, casting a significant look at Meredith. The vulnerable woman who'd sat on the edge of Meredith's bed watching Stacy nurse had disappeared, to be replaced by the hard, slightly catty woman who'd demanded more tequila in the margaritas.

Meredith stepped behind the bar and refilled the blender.

"That baby doesn't have the Brooks nose, does she, Kyle?" George quipped.

"Yes, Kyle. Confess. You weren't being naughty about a year ago, were you?" Rachel teased.

"Not guilty!" Kyle said. "This little girl's daddy is about to get slapped with a petition for support and back maintenance."

The high-pitched whir of the blender drew everyone's attention to the bar. After a few seconds, Meredith slapped the off switch. "Anyone for a fresh margarita?"

"I'll take one," Rachel spoke up.

After giving Rachel the drink, Meredith pointedly took Stacy from Kyle's arms. "Stacy's not used to all this confusion. I don't want her to get overtired."

She finished up in the kitchen, then wrapped Stacy in a blanket and carried her out to the screened porch. Meredith found the outside air refreshing as she stretched out on a lawn chaise and laid Stacy on her chest. From here, she could no longer hear the conversation in the living room, and that suited her just fine. Gazing at the sky, which was a deep indigo blue on this particular night, she pointed out a star and recited "Star Light, Star Bright" to her daughter.

"'I wish I may, I wish I might, have this wish I wish tonight.' Oh, Stacy," she murmured, hugging her daughter more tightly, "what happens when you want to wish that everything could be different from the way it is?"

Breathing in the clean baby scent of Stacy's head, she tilted her own head forward to kiss her and smiled sadly. "Not you, of course. I love you just the way you are. I wouldn't want you any different. But I'd sure want things to be different *for* you. I'd wish for you to be secure, and to always be surrounded by people who love you. But all you've got is me."

She swallowed. "But don't sell me short, kiddo. I'm tough, and I'll be here for you. You and I have come a long way, and we'll just keep right on going together."

Serenaded by the beating of her mother's heart, Stacy drifted to sleep, and Meredith lay still, listening to the crickets and Stacy's steady breathing. Meredith was nearly asleep when she was startled as she heard the door open.

"I didn't mean to disturb you," Kyle said, stepping onto the porch.

"I was just listening to the night."

"Rachel would like to talk to you."

"To me?"

Kyle clearly was not thrilled at the news he was carrying. "I can tell her you didn't want to be disturbed if you want me to."

"I'll talk to her. I just hope I can get upright without waking Stacy."

"I'll take her."

Meredith stiffened slightly as his hand slipped under Stacy's back and the back of his fingers brushed her breasts. Their eyes met—his filled with questions, and hers filled with pleas. He gently lifted Stacy. He handled her confidently now, quite differently than just weeks before, when he'd been awkward and unsure of himself around her. Nor did Stacy wake up as he carried her to her crib and gently rolled her onto her tummy. She was used to his touch, felt secure in his large, strong hands.

Meredith watched him lower Stacy into the crib and blinked back a tear of sadness. She could get used to that touch, too, would love to have the right to feel secure in Kyle's arms. But now one of his guests wanted to speak to his housekeeper.

Rachel's eyes were slightly glazed from the margaritas, but her speech was coherent. "I've decided to have a party," she announced. "A housewarming. In honor of my victory today. A few close friends to help me celebrate the exorcism of the creepoid."

"That sounds very lovely," Meredith said. *Was Rachel going to invite her to the party?*

"I need a caterer," Rachel continued. "And we were talking about it and I said wasn't it a shame that I didn't know anyone who could do the same kind of thing that you did for dinner tonight. And Kyle said that was interesting because you'd talked about becoming a caterer, and I asked if I could borrow you for the party."

"Borrow me?" Meredith made the words sound light in order to disguise her rage.

"You know, to cater my party. But Kyle—he's so cute, you know Kyle—he said he didn't *own* you and that you were free to do whatever you liked with your free time, but I had to ask you and cut my own deals."

"Yes. Kyle's cute that way, isn't he?" Meredith said, glowering at Kyle.

"So how about it? Next Saturday night. About fifty people?"

"Fifty close friends?"

Rachel missed the sarcasm. "Or sixty."

"I don't think so," Meredith replied. "I have my job here, and Stacy."

"Oh, please consider it," Rachel urged. "Kyle wouldn't mind if you let the laundry go a couple of days, would you Kyle? Make her say yes."

"Meredith makes her own decisions," Kyle told her.

Gee, thanks, Meredith thought. She looked at Rachel. "I don't—"

"Don't say no!" Rachel pleaded, holding up her hand like a crossing guard. "Think about it over the weekend, and I'll call you Monday to discuss it. I'm too drunk to talk about details now."

"All right," Meredith agreed, not wanting to antagonize Rachel. Maybe she'd forget the entire conversation when she sobered up. She looked at Kyle. "Should I make more margaritas before I go back to my quarters?"

Before Kyle could answer, Rachel picked up her goblet and drained it. Then, poising the stem between her thumb and forefinger, she flipped it back and forth. "My glass is emp-tee."

"Then we need more margaritas," Kyle said. He turned to Meredith, "Thank you for offering."

"Just doing my job," she answered pointedly.

After making the margaritas, she then retired to her quarters to read some back issues of a newsmagazine Kyle subscribed to. The occasional bursts of laughter from the living room were just distracting enough to keep her from falling asleep. Finally, a little after midnight, she heard the front door slam and the sound of an engine being started.

She was just reaching for the switch on the bedside lamp when a soft knock sounded at her door.

"Meredith?"

She opened the door about an inch and peered through the crack.

"I'd like to talk to you."

"It's late."

"Just for a few minutes."

She looked down at the tattered jersey she was using as a sleep shirt. What the hell? she decided. It wasn't glamorous, but you couldn't see through it and it reached almost to her knees. She had nothing to lose where Kyle was concerned; nothing to hide, for that matter. She opened the door and stepped into the kitchen.

Kyle looked ill at ease. "The buffet was perfect. Thank you for doing it on such short notice."

"What's a housekeeper for?"

"You looked very... *official*."

"White blouse, black skirt and apron," she explained. "Pretty basic. I was just relieved that the skirt buttoned."

Hesitantly Kyle said, "I know tonight wasn't easy for you."

"My, my, aren't you the sensitive one."

"Don't," he told her, reaching out to put his hands on her shoulders. She took a step back. Kyle sighed in defeat. "I just wanted you to know that I was proud of you."

"I'm sure it's gratifying having your guest of honor so impressed by the service that she asks to borrow your help."

"Don't confuse me with Rachel. I told her very quickly that you weren't mine to loan."

"Oh, yes, and when I was trying to decline that little job of hers, you were a lot of help."

"I said the decision was yours to make, not mine. It is. But, for the record, I think you should consider catering her party."

Shocked, Meredith asked, "You do?"

"You said you'd like to be a caterer. Rachel's party could be a good opportunity for you. She knows a lot of people who entertain."

"You must mean those fifty or sixty 'close friends.'"

"At least think about it. At worst, you'd make a little extra money. At best, it could lead to other parties."

"And I could be on my merry way a little sooner." It was out of her mouth before she realized how revealing it was.

It seemed that a long time passed before Kyle responded softly, "I'm not rushing you."

Silence. After another long pause, he said, "I just wanted to tell you that I was proud of the way you handled yourself."

"I wouldn't have wanted to be an embarrassment to you."

"It was my guests who were the embarrassment."

Meredith mulled over his words for several seconds. "Just tell me one thing, Kyle."

He cocked his head expectantly.

"Did you tell them that you slept with me?"

The expression on his face turned grim. She would have given anything to have taken back the question, but it was out, irretractable and hurtful.

"You ask me that?" he responded bitterly. A horrible silence followed. Finally, he turned and walked from the room.

Meredith watched him leave, wanting more than anything in the world to feel his arms around her.

13

MARK FOLDED HIS MENU and handed it to the waiter. "I'll have the twelve-ounce rib eye and a baked potato with the works."

"Watching your cholesterol?" Kyle teased. He'd ordered grilled chicken breast and spinach salad.

"I took vows of poverty and chastity, but I haven't conquered gluttony yet, especially when someone else is buying."

"I'm glad one of us has an appetite," Kyle replied.

"You know," Mark said, looking at Kyle over the rim of the glass of iced tea he'd just been served, "I was half expecting you to call."

"What? Are you clairvoyant now?"

"Hardly. But, then, I didn't have to be. Meredith called me earlier this week to ask if I knew anyone reliable who might be interested in baby-sitting for her on her day off. It seems she thought it was about time she started hunting for a different job."

He waited for Kyle to reply. Kyle didn't but the grave expression on his face was telling. Finally Mark prompted, "You don't seem too surprised."

"I told you the last time I talked to you that it wasn't working out."

"Ah, yes. Something about Meredith cooking muffins for breakfast and making sure the towels matched."

"It's worse than that."

"You've fallen in love."

"How did you know?"

Mark rolled his eyes. "What else gets two people so mixed up and miserable?"

"That's a fine attitude for a priest. I thought love was supposed to be the answer to everything."

"Often the very thing with the power to make you happiest also has the power to make you most miserable."

"Do they teach you that at the seminary?"

"Did you ask me here because you didn't have anyone else to eat with, or did you want advice?"

"I don't know what to do," Kyle confessed. To his consternation, Mark was grinning. "Do you find that amusing?" he asked irritably.

"I find it encouraging that you care enough about someone else to be miserable," Mark told him. "It's been a long journey, Kyle. Welcome back."

"You're talking in riddles."

"Am I? You've been in an emotional coma ever since—"

"Don't bring Shannon into this."

"You're going to have to deal with Shannon's death sooner or later, Kyle. The fact that you're able to care about another human being again is a sign you're finally ready to let go."

"You're crazy."

"Am I? When was the last time you truly cared about another human being?"

"I've built a successful legal practice caring about my clients."

"Have you? Or have you been vicariously punishing yourself by running roughshod over your clients' ex-husbands? You've been setting yourself up as avenger and meting out punishment in an effort to try to punish yourself for what happened to Shannon."

"Thank you, Father Freud."

"You weren't responsible for what happened to Shannon, Kyle."

"She was your *sister*," Kyle said. "You of all people should be willing to put blame where blame is due."

"Yes," Mark agreed. "She was my baby sister and I loved her. I was devastated when she died. I spent a lot of time praying for understanding. It would have been easy to blame you, Kyle, but the simple truth is that it wasn't your fault."

The waiter brought their food. Kyle waited until he'd put down their plates and was out of earshot before saying, "I shouldn't have let her leave when she was so upset."

"You didn't *let* Shannon do anything. If she left, it was because she wanted to leave. Look, Kyle, she was a human being, not a saint. A very headstrong human being. What happened was a tragic accident, pure and simple. She always had a lead foot. She had her first speeding ticket before her driver's license had cooled down from the laminating machine. When she got behind the wheel, she thought she was invincible." He paused to catch his breath and swallow a lump of emotion. "Plainly she wasn't."

The silence at the table was absolute.

"You've got to move forward," Mark said. "You've got to accept her death for what it was—a horrible accident."

Kyle was troubled enough over Meredith. Why was Mark insisting on talking about Shannon? "Why are you bringing all this up?" he asked.

"Look at who you've been the most ruthless with," Mark persisted. "Men who've hurt women—the way you thought you'd hurt Shannon."

"Even if there's a grain of truth in your theory—and I'm not conceding that there is—I don't see what it has to do with the way I feel about Meredith."

"Did you hear yourself just then?" Mark asked. "The way you *feel* about Meredith. You're *feeling* again. You've made your first step back, a giant step." Picking up his knife and fork, he sliced off a hefty chunk of beef and ate it appreciatively. "Delicious."

Kyle felt like punching Mark in the mouth for his obtuseness. He had yet to pick up his own eating utensils.

"The problem isn't that I can't *feel* for Meredith—I love her. The problem is that everything's so screwed up where she and I are concerned. Our relationship may be beyond redemption."

"No relationship built on genuine caring is beyond redemption," Mark replied, stirring the sour cream, chives and bacon bits into his potato.

"That's priest talk," Kyle said. "It's . . . the circumstances that are so convoluted. It may be just plain impossible."

"Nothing is impossible," Mark stated after swallowing a mouthful of potato.

Kyle didn't reply, didn't move. He still hadn't picked up his silverware.

Mark cut off another portion of steak. "If you don't feel like eating, why don't you tell me what's happened between the two of you that makes everything seem so hopeless."

Kyle told him, enduring Mark's disapproval when he confessed that he and Meredith had made love and then described her hostility afterward. He could hear Mark's unspoken censure.

He recounted his disastrous dinner party. "Things were bad enough already," he concluded miserably. "Then George came on to her like a lovesick fool and Rachel talked about 'borrowing' her as though she were a slave I'd bought on the auction block. And after they'd gone she wanted to know if I'd told them about—"

Mark swallowed and took a sip of tea. "And so now you think it's hopeless. It sounds to me more like your people skills are a little rusty."

"What the hell's that supposed to mean?"

"It means that you've gotten very good at sticking it to men in court, but you're out of practice with the one-on-one relationships."

"I haven't treated her badly."

"No one says you have."

"When we made love it was...I thought it had brought us close. But it seems to have driven us apart instead. So far that—"

"Was it truly lovemaking, or was it just good sex?"

Embarrassed, Kyle felt a flush creeping up his neck and over his cheeks. "That's a peculiar question coming from a priest."

"It wouldn't be so peculiar coming from Meredith, would it?"

Kyle shook his head. "No, but—"

"Suppose she asked it. What would you say?"

"That it was lovemaking. But she was there, surely she knew—"

"Did you *tell* her what it meant to you? What she means to you?"

"Not in so many words, but—"

"In *any* words?"

"No. But—"

"But what, Kyle. Did you think that because it was meaningful for you that she would mysteriously read your mind?"

"Have you forgotten what it's like to hold a woman, Mark? The feeling you get when you touch a woman or she touches you?"

"No. I haven't forgotten," he responded, adding wryly, "although at times my life would be easier if I had. I may not be involved in that particular game anymore," Mark conceded, "but my—shall we call it 'objective status'?—has helped me to learn a lot about women and relationships since I became a priest. I do a lot of counseling now. And the primary complaint I get from women is that men don't talk to them, don't share their feelings."

"Some things don't have to be said."

"From what I hear, the things men think *don't* need saying are the very things that *need* to be said the most. For instance, have you told Meredith that you felt you were making love and not just having sex?"

"She was there," Kyle stated. "She *had* to know."

"If she had been so sure that it was meaningful to you, would she have asked if you'd told your friends about it?"

Kyle paled.

"Look at it from her perspective, Kyle. Relationships work best when there's an assumption of equality. You're not only her boss, but you're her benefactor *and* her attorney. She's a servant, a charity case and a needy client, too. It would take a person of extraordinary strength not to feel *un*equal in her situation."

"Don't you think I know that? Why do you think I called you for advice? I know what the problem is. I don't know how to solve it."

"You might start by telling her how you feel."

"That would be disastrous at this point," Kyle said with conviction. "It would seem . . . artificial, and it would just complicate everything further."

"You'd have to be tactful," Mark conceded. "But the fact that you care about her is not a hurtful truth, it's a strengthening one."

"She's not ready for that pressure."

"You were working under the assumption that she already knew it."

Kyle frowned. "Instinctively. Not in a threatening, confront-her-with-the-news kind of way."

"Then perhaps you should focus your energy on what would make her ready to deal with it."

"I don't . . ." Kyle hesitated, shaking his head.

"What is your greatest fear where she's concerned?"

Kyle considered the question. "That I'll lose her. She's going to leave, Mark. She's talking about getting a different job and a place of her own. If she gets back maintenance from that yahoo she got involved with— and there's a good chance she will—then she's going to be gone so fast I'll get whiplash as she walks out the door. Right now she's scurrying around getting ready for that party she's catering, and that's going to give her the beginning of a move-out fund."

"What really scares you, Kyle? That she'll leave, or that she wouldn't be dependent on you anymore?"

"I don't want to lose her."

"Put yourself in her place, then. If you were Meredith, what would scare you most—being loved, or being dependent?"

Kyle paused thoughtfully. "Being dependent," he answered finally. "What happened to her has made her skittish. She's terrified of finding herself in the same situation again."

"Then maybe instead of worrying about her becoming independent enough to leave you, you should be directing your energy toward helping her become self-sufficient so she has the freedom to love you."

"What if I do that and she leaves and I lose her?"

"Do you want a relationship based on total dependency or one based on choice?"

Kyle was too agitated to answer.

Mark pressed on, "Do you want her to need you out of economic necessity, or to choose to be with you because she loves you?"

"I'd want her to love me, of course."

"Then you're going to have to put her needs above yours. You're going to have to help her gain the freedom to choose."

Kyle felt as though someone had knocked the wind out of him. "It's a gamble, Mark. My God, what a gamble."

Mark smiled slyly. "You're gambling on love. From my perspective, you couldn't ask for better odds."

He gave Kyle's untouched plate a disparaging look. "Eat your lunch, Kyle. I just caught sight of the dessert cart, and it looks like we're in for a near-religious experience."

14

KYLE WENT HOME half an hour earlier than usual and found Meredith at the kitchen table surrounded by recipe books and papers. "Working on Rachel's party?"

Meredith nodded, adding defensively, "I've already put dinner on."

Kyle smiled. "I don't have any complaints about your performance as housekeeper, Meredith. You've done an admirable job. I don't mind you taking some time to work on Rachel's party."

There was a hint of impatience in the way she sat looking up at him. He sat down at the table with her instead. "How's it going?"

"I've worked out the menu and now I'm putting together the shopping list. The real work comes on Saturday when I get to Rachel's house."

Kyle reached across the table and covered her hand with his, giving it a gentle squeeze as he smiled at her. "This is a great opportunity for you. Rachel's crowd does a lot of entertaining, and very few of them do their own dishes."

He pulled his hand away before she could read ulterior motives into the touch, but he felt triumphant that his message of support had been delivered and received. "Is there anything I can do to help you?"

Meredith drew in a weary sigh and released it. "No. So far my biggest problem seems to be finding a baby-sitter for Stacy. I got some names from Father Mark, but they're all either already busy Saturday, or they don't like to work at night."

"My receptionist has small children. Maybe I could get some recommendations from her."

"Stacy's so tiny."

"Let me ask. Next to you, Mitzi is the most conscientious mother I know. She wouldn't recommend anyone who wasn't reliable."

"It couldn't hurt, I suppose." She turned that gray gaze—the Meredith gaze—on him. "Thank you."

"What happens if you get other referrals?" he asked. "Will you try to start a catering business?"

"Not right away. It's too iffy."

"But it's what you want to do."

"I need a job with security and benefits. The catering would be a good sideline, for a little extra money."

The silence that fell between them was surprisingly comfortable. "Meredith," he said.

She turned the Meredith gaze on him again.

"The other night you asked me a question, and I responded in anger. I'd like to answer it now."

"Kyle—"

"The answer is no. I didn't tell my friends that we'd made love. It was too private. What we shared meant too much to me for me to talk about it with anyone else."

He pretended not to notice that her eyes were bright with tears. Of happiness? Of sadness? He didn't know, but he found it encouraging that their lovemaking had meant enough to her for her to react with such emotion. Standing, he said, "I'm going to—"

"Get out of your work clothes," she completed with a knowing grin. "I'll clean off the table so we can have dinner."

"Good," he replied. "I'm hungry. I didn't have much lunch." Suddenly he was ravenous.

SATURDAY WAS A BLUR of furious activity for Meredith. She spent the morning mixing sandwich fillings and dips and scrubbing and chopping vegetables at Kyle's house, then in the afternoon made vegetable sculptures and sandwiches in Rachel's kitchen.

Before the party, she made a quick run back to Kyle's to nurse Stacy, take a quick shower and change into her black skirt, white shirt and apron. She tied a black grosgrain ribbon into a bow at her neck and fluffed her hair in front of the mirror. She was pleased with the professional image she projected.

Mitzi had sent over her favorite and most reliable baby-sitter—her mother—and though leaving Stacy for the first time was difficult, it was easier, knowing that her baby was with someone so competent. When Meredith walked out of her bathroom, Mrs. Stillman was bouncing Stacy in her lap with a practiced air while singing "Who Put the Bop in the Bop-She-Bop-She-Bop?"

"I'll be back as early as possible," Meredith told her for the third time. Mrs. Stillman hardly stalled between "she-bops" to assure her—for the tenth time—that she didn't have a thing to worry about.

Meredith was halfway to the side door when the front doorbell rang. Thinking it was probably the parcel deliveryman who had a late-afternoon route in the neighborhood, she discovered instead a middle-aged woman in a seersucker coverall with the logo of a local florist on the breast pocket.

"Meredith?" the woman asked.

Dumfounded, Meredith nodded.

"These are for you, then. Can you sign for them please?"

Meredith couldn't believe her eyes. Carnations, roses and baby's breath! She hadn't had flowers since her corsage for the senior prom. She carried the bouquet to the dining-room table and ripped open the envelope.

Just be your usual efficient self and you'll be the talk of the town. Kyle.

It was *exactly* what she needed. What a man! What woman wouldn't have fallen in love with him?

She took one of the carnations with her to Rachel's for luck, but hardly had time to think of it as the party got under way and all her attention went to keeping the trays of food full and attractive-looking while fifty of Rachel's "nearest and dearest" friends munched and crunched their hungry way through the results of all her work.

She saw Kyle a few times during the evening. He was always surrounded by people. When he made a deliberate detour into the kitchen to tell her the party was going splendidly and the food was delicious, she finally managed to thank him for the flowers.

Embarrassed to have been caught in a blatantly sentimental gesture, he kissed her on the cheek and told her he'd see her back at the house.

It was about one in the morning when Meredith returned, exhausted and exhilarated, to Kyle's. She was alarmed to see that Mrs. Stillman's car was gone, momentarily panicking until she noticed Kyle's car in the garage and surmised that Stacy was sleeping and Kyle had sent Mrs. Stillman home.

Kyle was waiting for her in the kitchen.

"Stacy?" she inquired, making a beeline toward her quarters.

"Sleeping peacefully," Kyle said. By the time he replied, she'd tiptoed up to Stacy's crib to see for herself. She looked at her, kissed her lightly on the cheek to check that she had no fever, and listened for the sound of even breathing.

Kyle, who'd followed her, cupped her elbow in his hand. She gave him a questioning look, and he put his finger to his lips to shush her and bobbed his head toward the door. In the living room Kyle had left a wine bottle in a bucket of ice.

"What's this?" Meredith asked.

"A celebration of your success," he explained.

"What did you hear?" she asked. "What were people really saying?"

"That the food was delicious and the centerpieces were beautiful."

"Really?" she persisted.

"Cross my heart," Kyle assured her, drawing an X across his chest.

"Two people asked Rachel who her caterer was and how to contact me," she reported excitedly. "A golden wedding anniversary and a fortieth birthday party. They may not work out, of course, but if they do—"

"They will," Kyle said confidently. "Which is why we're celebrating." He lifted the bottle from the ice bucket. "First, though, I want you to sit down and prop up your feet while I open and pour."

"Just a tiny sip for me," she warned—regretfully, because she didn't want to spoil the mood. "I'm nursing, remember?"

"That's why," he explained, dramatically turning the label so she could read it, "it's sparkling grape juice instead of champagne."

Touched by his thoughtfulness, Meredith laughed aloud. Kyle poured the juice, then handed her a goblet. His fingertips touched hers as he transferred the glass to her hand. He raised his own glass and looked into her eyes. "To success, and the launch of a new sideline."

They clinked glasses. For an instant, Meredith felt as if she had wandered into a movie about sophisticated, debonair people. It was almost *too* romantic to be real. But the glass was smooth against her lips, the sparkling grape juice was tart on her tongue, and the expression in Kyle's eyes as he looked at her face was too warm for fantasy.

"Aren't you proud of yourself?" he asked, and she nodded. "Good," he said, smiling. "You should be."

The expression in his eyes grew warmer; it warmed Meredith from the inside out. He was going to kiss her, and she was going to let him. In fact, she could hardly wait.

It would have happened, she was certain, if Stacy hadn't woken up at that moment and begun crying. Poised on the edge of the sofa, Meredith listened to see if her crying would wind down or crank up.

It cranked up.

Meredith stood. "I'm sorry. I'll have to feed her."

"Sit back down. I'll bring her to you."

"Kyle."

"I want your company a while longer," he said, and grinned. "I won't peep."

Stacy's crying got louder. "Go on," he urged on his way out of the room. "Sit back. Get comfortable. Your daughter's on her way."

Meredith did as she was told. There was a special tenderness in the way he laid Stacy in her arms a minute later—a reverence for her and Stacy that moved her. She waited for Kyle to sit down in his big easy chair, then unbuttoned her blouse and folded back the cup of her bra so Stacy could nurse.

She felt replete. The mood and the moment were special: here was Stacy, still small enough to need her; Kyle, celebrating with her; and the comfort and security of being in a home.

She looked over at Kyle, who was watching her intently.

"It's not what you think," he said. "The two of you—"

Meredith understood what he meant. He felt connected to them both, and shared their contentment.

He moved to sit next to her on the couch and put his arm around her. Gradually she eased into the natural cradle of his shoulder. It was a heavenly sensation, resting against Kyle, with Stacy nestled at her breast, suckling.

"What does it feel like when she does that?" he asked.

Meredith laughed softly. "That's like asking what a kiss feels like. It just . . . It feels pleasant and warm, and it gives me a good feeling inside, because I know I'm giving her something that no one else can give her. It feels safe, because while she's here, this close to me, I can be sure she's okay. When I feel her moving, some of the movements are familiar, because I remember her moving inside me. And she feels some of the same things. She hears my heartbeat and remembers the sound of it."

"I think you're beautiful," Kyle said. "Both of you. Together."

After a few minutes, she moved Stacy to the other breast and shifted to stretch herself out full length, with her head in Kyle's lap. Later, when Stacy had finished nursing, Kyle lifted the baby and held her on his shoulder while Meredith rebuttoned her blouse.

Before long, both mother and daughter were asleep; but Kyle was wide awake—wide awake and filled with hope.

15

"I FILED THE PAPERS," Kyle announced.

"You waited all weekend to tell me, didn't you?" Meredith said, her tone slightly accusatory. It was late Sunday afternoon and they were having milk shakes in Schwab's Drugstore at Universal Studios in Orlando after spending the day encountering movie ghosts, giant gorillas and great white sharks.

"I couldn't see any purpose in having you worry about it while you were preoccupied with Rachel's party."

Her expression tense, Meredith didn't comment.

"You hate this whole business, don't you?" Kyle asked.

"It seems so . . . manipulative, so invasive. Thomas has made it clear how he feels about Stacy. And me."

In her voice Kyle could hear the pain that lingered from Castor's betrayal of her, his brutal rejection of her and his denial of Stacy.

He'll pay, Kyle vowed silently. *For hurting Meredith and denying Stacy, Thomas Castor will pay dearly.*

"He is her father," he told Meredith, glancing at Stacy, who was sleeping soundly in a rented stroller. "He has a legal obligation to support her. You owe it to her to make him live up to that obligation."

"You can't turn an insensitive jerk into a human being by filing a lawsuit."

"We don't have to turn him into a human being. We just have to make him live up to his legal obligations."

Meredith sighed. "We've been over this before."

He nodded. *More than once.* And he suspected they would never see eye to eye on this issue.

"When will we hear something?"

"That depends on when the papers are served and how Castor wants to play it."

"So we just wait."

"That's about the size of it."

So they waited. Nine tense days. During that time Meredith lived in a state of nervous expectancy. She wondered at times how she would have endured the waiting if Kyle hadn't been so sweet to her, so optimistic, so quick to reassure her that she was doing the right thing.

Despite his reassurances, though, she kept remembering the hard look on Thomas's face when she'd told him she was pregnant, remembering his callous accusation that she was trying to pawn some other man's baby off on him. She had seen and heard enough irrationality and hostility in him for her to be skeptical about his agreeing to support the child he had told her he'd pay to get rid of.

She had a nightmare about him one night—a vision of him, his face distorted in anger, as he stalked her threateningly. She woke up in a cold sweat, gasping for breath, and raced to Stacy's crib to reassure herself that her baby was all right.

But her nightmare did not prepare her for the reality of finding Thomas on the doorstep two mornings later. He rang the doorbell, briskly pushed past her when she opened the door, and was in the house before she'd managed to blurt out his name.

"Where is she?" he demanded.

"Who?"

"Don't play coy with me. I'm talking about our daughter. The bundle of joy you want to stick me with."

"Thomas!" she pleaded. He was beyond reason, dashing from room to room.

"You can't do this," she begged. After exhausting the bedrooms at the back of the house, he entered the living room, getting too close to her quarters and Stacy, who was asleep in the crib.

"You think not?" he challenged. "Why can't I see my darling little daughter? After all, I was just sitting in my office doing my job when a uniformed deputy brought me the news that I'm being sued for child support and back maintenance."

Thomas's rage terrified her, as did the prospect of him finding Stacy. She had to talk some sense into him and get him to leave. Gesturing toward the sofa, she implored, "Why don't you sit down, Thomas. We can talk about this calmly."

"Oh, no, sweetheart. We tried talking months ago. I told you what I thought you ought to do, but you didn't listen to me. Then you did your talking to a lawyer."

"I'm sorry it had to be done that way," she said. "Why don't we—"

"Where is she?" he demanded.

Meredith didn't respond.

"You're not the only person who can get an attorney, you know. I've got one. He tells me we all have to go in for blood tests, just in case you're trying to pull a fast one. How do you suppose they take blood from a baby, Meredith? Are you going to watch them do it?"

"You know she's yours!" Meredith retorted, finally giving way to her anger. "You know there was no one else!"

"Back in Indiana," Thomas corrected. "But that was before you moved in with your lawyer, sweetheart. My attorney thought your address sounded *exclusive*, and guess what the crisscross turned up. You're *living* here with him!"

"I'm his housekeeper."

He sneered. "Is that what you're calling it?"

"I was *homeless*, Thomas. Your daughter—*your daughter*—and I were living in the car. You wouldn't help us. When I got offered a job as a housekeeper, I jumped at it."

"Yeah. I guess so. I can see where this little setup beats working a street corner on the Trail. And you got an attorney who's going to stick me with child support in the bargain."

His callousness still had the power to shock her. This was a man she'd thought she knew, a man she'd loved. How could she have been so wrong about him?

He took several steps toward the kitchen. She ran after him, grabbed at his arm to stop him, but he shook her away.

"What's wrong, Momma? Am I getting close? I have rights, you know. I have an attorney, too. If I get to be the papa with a checkbook, then I can ask for visitation rights. Wouldn't want to neglect my *kin*. I might as well start getting acquainted right now."

"No," Meredith insisted, tears of fear and frustration stinging her eyes. "Thomas, you can't—"

He kept searching, pausing when he spied Stacy's empty infant seat on the work island. "I am close," he said. "Let's see. Maybe if I call her."

"Please," Meredith begged. She'd lost the battle with her tears and they were streaming down her cheeks.

Thomas looked offended. "What's wrong, Mommy? Haven't you heard that turnabout is fair play? I'm not dumb enough to pay for something I don't get to enjoy."

"Not this way, Thomas," she pleaded. "Wait until you calm down. She's so tiny."

He'd spied the crib through the half-open door to her quarters, and he let her know it with a hideous smile of triumph. "She's not too little to know her daddy now, is she? Never too young for that."

He was beside the crib before she could take a breath.

"No!" she cried out. Maternal instinct propelled her forward and she grabbed his arm, trying to pull him away, but he shook her off like a pesky insect.

She watched in horror as he lifted Stacy out of the crib and, holding her under the arms, dangled her in front of his face. The total lack of caring she saw in his features terrified her.

Rudely wrested from sound sleep, Stacy wailed, but he ignored her. "Who do you look like?" he asked. "Do you look like me or the mailman?"

"Put her down, Thomas."

The bone-chilling tone of her voice made Thomas lower Stacy into the crib. Meredith scurried over. Pushing Thomas aside, she picked up Stacy, who was screaming. "Get out of here!" she told him. "If you don't leave, I'm going to call the cops."

Thomas gave her a twisted smile. "I'll leave. But I'm not going to roll over and play dead. If I acknowledge paternity, I may just decide to become a papa full-time."

Meredith stared at him from above Stacy's head. What he was hinting at was too ludicrous for comprehension.

He smirked. "You haven't proved yourself to be a good provider, have you? Living in the car. Living here with a man under questionable circumstances."

"I've taken care of her," she defended. "I'd die for her. You didn't even want her."

"I'm engaged to be married," he countered. "I've got a good job, a beautiful fiancée. She doesn't know about this yet, but...who knows? She's crazy about kids. We might decide to sue for custody."

"You wanted me to *kill* her! No judge in the world would give her to you after—"

He made a tut-tut sound with his tongue and shook his head with mock sadness. "Judges look at what's right for the kid, Meredith. Look at it objectively. I've got a great job, my wife and I could give her a stable home environment. You—"

He shook his head again. "Homeless. Then, living with a man, calling yourself a housekeeper. As for what I said or did before she was born, it would be my word against yours. Who do you think the judge would believe?"

"You'll never get her. Do you hear me? I'll never give her up."

"You could drop the suit," he suggested. "If you dropped the suit, then you wouldn't have to worry. Without blood tests, there's no proof she's mine, so there'd be nothing I could do about her."

After pausing for dramatic effect, he said hatefully, "Think about it, sweetheart."

Meredith stood frozen in place until she heard the front door slam. Then she grabbed the diaper bag and her purse and ran to the car with Stacy in her arms. She had to get to Kyle and get him to drop the suit. She couldn't let Thomas touch Stacy again, wouldn't take a chance on him getting her.

While stopped at a red light, she fished one of Kyle's business cards from her purse with trembling fingers. She knew his office was downtown, but she'd never been there. How long would it take her to get there? It seemed an eternity, but the dashboard clock told her only twelve minutes had passed before she found the right exit and then the right street. Chanting the street number over and over like a litany, she found the right building, then searched desperately for a parking space.

Where were the quarters in her coin purse for the parking meter? Why wouldn't the elevator come? She finally dashed up the two flights of stairs to the third level of the office building and then searched frantically for his suite.

"I have to see Kyle—immediately," she told his receptionist.

Mitzi reached for the telephone on her desk. "I'll see—"

Meredith dashed past the desk into the hallway that led to the inner offices.

"Excuse me," the receptionist called after her. "Excuse me, you can't just—"

"Is he here?" Meredith asked, reaching for the knob of a door that looked promising.

"You can't—"

But Meredith was already in. Kyle was seated behind a huge desk. His face registered alarm when he caught sight of her. "Meredith," he said, standing.

"I've got to talk to you."

Mitzi had followed on Meredith's heels and was staring at Kyle. "I've called Security."

"Call them back. Tell them it's a false alarm," Kyle told her.

The attorney he'd been talking to stood also, and gave Kyle a questioning look.

"Can you excuse us for a few minutes?" Kyle asked him. "Mitzi, why don't you show Mr. Phelps where the coffeepot is."

Cupping Meredith's elbow, he propelled her down the hall and through a door, which he closed behind them. She was in his arms instantly, with Stacy caught in the middle of the hug. "Castor?" he asked.

"How did you know?"

"Stacy doesn't seem to be in any trouble. What else would make you tremble so."

"He came to the house. He picked Stacy up. He woke her up and scared her. He says if we make him pay support, then he has a right to ask for visitation. He said he would sue for custody."

They were in a conference room with a long table and padded leather chairs. Kyle guided her into a chair and sat down next to her, holding her free hand. "It was a ploy, Meredith. He's just trying to intimidate you. His attorney called today to set up an appointment for tomorrow afternoon."

"I want to drop the suit."

"That's absurd. He's bluffing. If you drop the suit now, then you're doing exactly what he wants." He could see the fear in her eyes.

"It's true, isn't it? If we ask for child support and win, he can ask for visitation rights. If we make him acknowledge paternity, he could sue for custody."

"He could. But what makes you think he'd want to, with the attitude he's shown toward her?"

"Because he has to win. You didn't see him, Kyle. He said he's not going to pay for something he can't enjoy. He said his fiancée is crazy about kids, and that he could give her a more secure home than I can."

"He's preying on your fears, Meredith."

"I can't take that chance. I'd rather—"

"You'd rather lie down and let him walk all over you. You'd rather be a victim and give up than assert your rights and fight for what's yours. He's not going to get custody of Stacy even if he tries."

"Oh, Kyle, you didn't see him! You didn't hear him! If he decides he wants Stacy, he'll win. He'll lie, and the judge will give Stacy to him because he's got a steady job and he's getting married."

Kyle stood and paced the floor a few times before stopping in front of her. "You've got to trust me," he said. "As someone who cares about you, and as your attorney."

"As your client, I'm asking you to drop the suit."

"I can't do that."

"Can't—or won't?"

"It's not in your best interests or Stacy's to drop the suit."

"You're talking like a lawyer," she told him. "I'm a mother. Kyle, can't you see that I can't take that chance?"

"You have to. You can't buckle under at the first show of force."

"What would I do if he sued for custody and won? What would it do to Stacy?"

"The odds of that happening are one in a hundred."

"You're talking to me about odds? Kyle, I wouldn't care if it was one in a million. People buy lottery tickets on slimmer odds than that. I can't take *any* chance."

"We've got to talk to his attorney, at least. Castor's angry now. When he cools down and listens to counsel, he'll come around. Let's not make any rash decisions before we even hear what his attorney has to say."

Meredith was quivering but defiant. "My decision was made the moment Thomas touched Stacy. He's never going to touch her again, Kyle. I won't let it happen. He doesn't *deserve* to touch her."

"And you don't deserve to be stuck with full responsibility for a child that has two parents. You've come a long way, Meredith. Don't cave in now."

Her breathing was ragged, her voice strained. "You don't understand, do you? All you see is the *law*, and *legal* obligation. Look at me, Kyle. Look at my face. Look at Stacy's face. Don't you see us? Don't you see that this is about *us*, and not about legal issues?"

He knelt beside her, touched her hair and then Stacy's head. "You're upset. We don't have to make any decision right this moment. Tomorrow I'll talk to Castor's attorney and then we can make an informed decision together."

"If, after tomorrow, I still want to drop the suit, will you do it?"

"If I don't feel that I can in good conscience drop the suit, and you insist on dropping it, then I'll resign from the case, and you'll be free to do or not do anything you like about Castor."

Meredith nodded gravely. She understood the implied message. If Kyle resigned from the case, it would be the end of any chance for them. They'd been making progress, growing closer, but the issue that separated them had reared its head again. She was the willing victim; he was the advocate of absolute justice.

He took her hand again. "Are you all right now?"

She just stared at him. *All right? She might never be all right again if he and Thomas had their way.*

Kyle glanced at his watch. "I can tie up the consultation I was in in about fifteen minutes and then I'm through for the day. Why don't you wait for me, and I'll follow you home so you don't have to go back into the house by yourself."

Too tired to argue, she nodded.

"I'll have Mitzi bring you a soft drink."

Again she nodded, thinking as she did so that it was going to take more than a soft drink to settle her nerves.

By the time she turned into Kyle's driveway an hour later, she was ready to retreat to her quarters.

But while she waited at the door for Kyle to walk from the garage, she heard Champ meowing. Sighing, Meredith turned, ready to kneel and pet the cat.

Then she caught sight of Champ. He was limping and bloody. "Oh, Champ!" she groaned. "Why today?"

"What happened to him?" Kyle asked.

Meredith scowled at him. "*This* is why you neuter male cats."

"Don't blame me," Kyle said. "I'm only the land-lord."

"Well, landlord, open the door so I can put Stacy in her crib. We've got to clean those wounds."

"Are you serious?"

"After the day I've had, I couldn't be anything but serious."

She walked into her quarters carrying Stacy and came out seconds later, armed to fight infection. Kyle followed her outside.

"Where are you going?" she asked.

"You're going to need some help controlling that beast or you'll wind up in worse shape than he is."

"I'm already in worse shape than he is. It just doesn't show."

Loosely grabbing her wrist, Kyle spoke her name. She looked up at him. "What now?"

"You're not alone," he said.

Sighing, she sagged against him as he drew her into his arms and kissed the top of her head. "I don't know why Champ had to pick today to go out philander-ing."

"Love knows no timing," Kyle explained, releasing her when Champ limped over to them and meowed weakly.

"I thought animals cleaned their own wounds," Kyle remarked, kneeling beside her as she sat down, scooped Champ into her lap and wrapped him in the towel. "Don't they lick themselves or something?"

With exasperation, Meredith said, "Show me a cat that can lick his own ear and I'll show you an elephant that can juggle."

"Point conceded," Kyle replied. "What do we do?"

She tossed Kyle the cotton balls and peroxide. "Saturate these and dab."

She murmured assurances to Champ while Kyle worked.

He was gentle but efficient. "These don't look all that serious," he announced after he'd finished one ear and started on the other. "Just shallow puncture wounds. Teeth marks." He spoke to Champ. "I hope you gave 'em as good as you got, old boy."

"Oh, great! Encourage him."

"Me? He doesn't need encouragement from me! You can bet there was a female at the bottom of this, egging them on."

Meredith examined Champ and saw that all his wounds were superficial, so when he grew impatient, Meredith let him go.

She turned to Kyle. "Thanks for helping."

"He's not so bad—for a cat."

Meredith smiled. "He likes you, too."

Sitting there next to each other on the narrow strip of grass between the driveway and the porch, they fell into a comfortable silence. Kyle wrapped his hand around hers and gave it a gentle squeeze. "We'll have a better idea about what to do about the suit tomorrow."

"I know what to do about the suit," she said. "It's you who's uncertain."

Their rapport now shattered, Meredith gathered up the used cotton balls and took them to the trash. Kyle followed her into the house.

She walked to the door of her quarters and paused. "I'm not hungry and it's been a long day. Do you mind—?"

"I can manage," he replied. "I know you've got a lot on your mind. Get some rest."

He stared at the door after she closed it, then went into the kitchen to make himself a sandwich. He found himself looking at her door as he ate, missing her company.

He tried to shake the image of her bursting into his office, trembling and terrified, and couldn't. He wanted to squeeze Thomas Castor until he cried for mercy.

And Meredith wanted to drop the case. It irked him that she was so easily manipulated, that she would let Castor's terrorist tactic intimidate her. How could a woman with the strength he'd seen in her just roll over and play dead?

He knew with every iota of attorney's instinct—hell, with every ounce of common sense he possessed—that she shouldn't drop the suit. Yet she was closed-minded on the subject. Which left him in a dilemma. Did he go against his instincts and drop the suit in order to please her? Or did he fight for her the way he knew he should?

What happened if he won his client generous child support terms but wound up losing the woman he loved in the process? She was asking him to compromise what he knew to be right as an attorney in favor of what he felt to be right as a mother. Sleep eluded him that night, as he tossed and turned, mulling over the dilemma.

He'd just checked the lighted dial of the bedside clock for the third time—it was 3:28 a.m.—when he heard footsteps on the hall carpet. A gentle knock followed.

"Meredith?" he asked.

She stepped into the room, a shadowy figure in a stretched-out football jersey holding Stacy in her arms.

"I couldn't sleep," she whispered.

"I'm not doing such a good job of it myself."

"I keep thinking about tomorrow."

"Me, too."

"I don't want to be alone."

Kyle laid his head back on his pillow and sighed. "We could play gin rummy, I suppose."

"I don't know how."

"I'm not even sure I own a deck of cards." He flung out his arm, tossing the covers back invitingly. "We could hold each other."

She hesitated. "Stacy, too?"

"Especially Stacy."

They spent the night cuddled together in his bed, and when Kyle's alarm rang, he had to reach across Meredith and Stacy to cut it off.

He watched Meredith open her eyes—those gray eyes. They were bigger and more expressive in the morning light than he'd ever seen them. He looked at Stacy nestled in her mother's arms.

"I'll do what's best for everyone today," he promised.

"You'll drop the suit?"

"I'll do what's best."

She closed her eyes and sighed sadly.

16

MEREDITH CHECKED the clock for the fourth time in fifteen minutes. Kyle was late. Why hadn't he called after talking to Thomas's attorney?

She watched the door even more closely than she watched the clock. *Please, Kyle, walk through that door and tell me you dropped the suit. Tell me you didn't gamble on Stacy's and my future.*

Finally there came the sound of tires on pavement and the hum of an engine. Meredith stood in the middle of the kitchen, her attention focused on the door when he entered.

Kyle looks tired. The knot of his tie had slipped down several inches and the collar of his shirt was open.

He went through his nightly routine, putting his portfolio on the desk, checking the answering machine for messages. There were none, of course; Meredith had not left the house all day.

His eyes met Meredith's. "We have to talk."

"Did you drop the suit?"

He didn't respond. Instead, he walked to her and opened his arms. "Come here, Meredith."

She stepped forward and slid her arms around his waist. With her cheek against his chest she listened to the beating of his heart, drawing strength from its rhythm. "Tell me," she implored softly.

Dropping one arm, he left the other draped across her shoulders and guided her into the living room. "Sit down," he said. "There's no reason we can't be comfortable."

"What happened?" she pressed.

"Castor came with his attorney."

"Did you drop the suit?"

"I wanted to hurt him," Kyle answered distractedly. "It wasn't simply that I wanted to stick it to him with child support, I wanted to *hurt* him."

He turned to Meredith. "It scared me—the strength of my need to inflict pain. He introduced himself and held out his hand for me to shake it and suddenly I thought, He touched Stacy with that hand. And I wanted to hit him. I wanted to punish him for everything he'd done to you and everything he'd failed to do for you, and for what he'd wanted to do to Stacy."

Meredith felt like screaming in frustration but she let him continue at his own pace. Kyle was plainly upset by his overreaction to Thomas.

"When I finished shaking hands with him, I dropped my right arm to my side and formed a fist with my hand and I thought, He made love to Meredith. He made her love him. It would have been so easy to cram his teeth down into his Adam's apple."

"You didn't—?"

"No. It was tempting, but I realized in the nick of time that all hitting him would accomplish would be to land my butt in jail and lose my license."

"What about the suit?"

"I listened to what they had to say, and it was pretty much what I expected. They wanted a blood test to determine whether Castor could be ruled out as the father of the baby."

"Kyle, please. The suspense is killing me. What did you do?"

"I made sure Castor will never come near you or Stacy again."

"You dropped the suit?"

"I went one better. In exchange for our dropping the suit, Castor signed an agreement never to seek out Stacy or attempt to claim any parental rights. In addition, he agreed that in the event you should marry, your husband would, at your discretion, be free to adopt Stacy."

"Adopt?"

"When I realized that that piece of slime had *touched* Stacy after refusing to help you when he knew the two of you were destitute, I realized that Stacy *would* be better off without him in her life. And that she deserved a father who loved her, and who wanted to watch her grow up and be a part of her life—"

His eyes met Meredith's. "And I realized that *I* loved her, and that I want to watch her grow up and be a part of her life, just as I love her mother and want to be a part of her mother's life."

He reached for Meredith's hand. "I know this is sudden and it's less than romantic but— Damn it, Meredith, I love you and I love Stacy, and I know we can be happy."

Meredith was too struck for words.

"Marry me," he said. "You can finish your degree and start a catering business and have another couple of kids and Stacy can call me Daddy because I *will* be her daddy."

She was still speechless.

"It wouldn't be just a marriage of convenience. I love you, and eventually—"

"You brilliant, adorable, gallant idiot!" she exclaimed. "If you say I could grow to love you, *I'm* going to knock *your* teeth down *your* Adam's apple."

It was Kyle's turn to be at a loss for words.

"I already love you," Meredith told him. "I just was afraid . . . It didn't seem possible that . . ."

He kissed her, gently at first and then passionately. "I wanted to tell you after we made love, but it was so new. And then when you were so angry—"

"Because I wanted you to love me the way I loved you, and I didn't think you did—"

"And you talked about getting a job and moving out—"

"This was always supposed to be temporary. I knew the whole housekeeper thing was just a polite way of giving me a home until I got my strength back. I couldn't go on being a charity case forever, and when I fell in love with you, it just rushed the timetable. I knew I couldn't go on being around you without you realizing that I loved you. And there was Stacy—"

"Stacy?"

"She was getting attached to you. I was afraid if we stayed much longer that it would be traumatic for her when we left."

"I want to adopt her," he said. "I can't be her biological father, but I want to be a father to her in every other way."

Meredith had settled in his arms, with her head on his shoulder. She laughed softly. "You were so funny the first time you held her. So stiff."

"And she went to sleep on my shoulder anyway."

"Who could blame her?" Meredith replied, burrowing her cheek against him contentedly.

Kyle kissed the top of her head. "Will you marry me?"

"Yes."

They held each other quietly, contentedly. Then Meredith asked, "Why did you agree to let me and

Stacy live here? It was because of something between you and Father Mark, wasn't it?"

"Yes." He paused to collect and sort his thoughts before continuing. "Mark and I have been friends for a long time. Since grammar school. He had a kid sister, Shannon. She was a real pest most of the time, always hanging around. But then…suddenly…while we were away at college, she grew up. And one summer we went home and—"

He kissed the top of Meredith's head. "She wasn't a kid anymore. And she wasn't *my* sister. So we dated, and by the time I finished law school, we were engaged."

"What happened?"

"We were planning the wedding and everything got…crazy. I took a long lunch to go to the formal-wear store with her. She'd picked out a tux for me, but I wanted something simpler. We argued about it all the way back to my office, and then argued about it some more. We'd have kept on arguing if I hadn't had an appointment I couldn't break. I was just getting the practice started and every client was important."

Feeling him tense, Meredith took his hand and kissed it.

"She left angry. Because of the tuxedo, and because I wouldn't cancel my appointment to go over what we'd already been over. It was raining outside. One of those sudden afternoon showers that they call 'Florida ice,' when oil floats up out of the asphalt after a light rain. She hit a patch and—"

He took a breath. "She never made it home. The cops said she was doing fifty around a curve with a posted twenty-five-miles-per-hour speed. It was an accident, of course, but I kept seeing her the way she was when she left the office, so upset."

"You blamed yourself," Meredith said softly.

"If I'd just stopped her. If I'd canceled my stupid appointment. If I'd just agreed to wear that stupid tuxedo—"

"You couldn't have known what was going to happen," Meredith told him.

"I know. And Shannon drove like a bat out of hell. Everyone always told her she was going to end up wrapped around a tree." He paused. "It was a light pole instead."

"Did Father Mark blame you for what happened?"

"No. But I blamed myself, and I didn't realize until today..."

He smiled down at Meredith's face. "It seems to be a day for realizations, doesn't it?"

"What else did you realize besides the fact that you're madly in love with me?"

"Mark says I've been punishing men who mistreat women because I couldn't forgive myself for what I thought I did to Shannon. And today, with Castor, I realized Mark was right. I hadn't cared about all those women I'd helped—not really. I'd just been making men pay on principle. But today—today I felt what I was feeling because of you and Stacy. I saw your faces when I looked at him, and I wanted to kill him. And I had to let go of that anger in order to protect you. It came down to a choice between principle and love, and I made the civilized choice. Who knows? Maybe there's hope for me as a human being."

Meredith wrapped her arms around his neck and kissed him. "Was there ever any doubt?"

He clung to her, holding her against him. "Oh, yes. There was doubt."

"You took in a homeless woman and her child. I think that speaks well for your human compassion."

"You were never *home*less, Meredith. Not the way you love Stacy, the way you care for her. You just didn't have a *house*. I had a house, but it wasn't a home. Until you and Stacy moved in."

Meredith blinked back a tear. "It sounds as though we should combine assets."

"Permanently," he added, and kissed her.

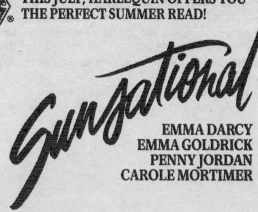

Harlequin Superromance®

CHILDREN OF THE HEART
by Sally Garrett

Available this August

Romance readers the world over have wept and
rejoiced over Sally Garrett's heartwarming stories of
love, caring and commitment. In her new novel,
Children of the Heart, Sally once again weaves a story
that will touch your most tender emotions.

You'll be moved to tears of joy

Nearly two hundred children have passed through
Trenance McKay's foster home. But after her husband
leaves her, Trenance knows she'll always have to
struggle alone. No man could have enough room in his
heart both for Trenance and for so many needy
children. Max Tulley, news anchor for KSPO TV is
willing to try, but how long can his love last?

"Sally Garrett does some of the best character studies
in the genre and will not disappoint her fans."
Romantic Times

**Look for *Children of the Heart* wherever
Harlequin Romance novels are sold.** SCH-1